CYCLING

A SOURCE BOOK

Philip Ennis

A SOURCE BOOK

PELHAM BOOKS
London

First published in Great Britain by
PELHAM BOOKS LTD
44 Bedford Square
London WC1B 3DU
1984

British Library Cataloguing in Publication Data

Ennis, Philip
Cycling
1. Cycling
I. Title
796.6   GV1041

ISBN 0-7207-1496-6

Typeset by Rowland Phototypesetting Ltd,
Bury St Edmunds, Suffolk
Printed and bound in Great Britain by
Hollen Street Press Ltd, Slough, Bucks

CONTENTS

PREFACE

Cycling continues to grow in popularity, as sport, pastime and means of transport. Every year there are more races and types of races, more organised rides and types of rides, more clubs and associations, more cycles and accessories, more cyclists. It is expanding and ever evolving.

Letters in the cycling press, sometimes from experienced cyclists, reveal that many are bewildered by the sheer complexity of it all. Listen to the racing cyclist Dave Cahill:

> 'There I was, ready to hang up my wheels and retire from my beloved sport. And then John Nicholas wrote an article on AUDAX(UK). What a wonderful way of competing! My interest in cycling was renewed.
>
> But wait. I've read the article by Tim Hughes; now he must be right. We don't want restrictions and time limits. No, it's back on the bike and ride his way. Oh, heck! Now I've turned the page. Joe Mummery must be right. It's faster we go. Get on the drag strips, take a lift from a lorry . . .
>
> All I can say is, "Help! I'm going round the bend." '
>
> (*Cycling* 26 March 1980)

Dave is not simply highlighting a trio of opinions but articulating a little of the despair of the present-day cyclist. There is so much going on, it is not only impossible to take part in everything, but difficult to comprehend it all.

This book seeks to throw light on the cycling scene. It is a source book which I hope will be of use to the absolute beginner – whether racing, touring or commuting – yet contain much for the experienced cyclist.

I have tried to provide, within the severe limits of space, a comprehensive overview, though not exhaustive. Information is given to stimulate, to whet the appetite, to feed enthusiasms.

A significant part of the book is devoted to clubs and organisations. It was while collecting information for this chapter that the wealth of friendship in cycling circles was brought home to me. I received so much fascinating material from club secretaries – some of which must have taken hours to prepare – that ten books could be written. I know they will understand that lack of space only has precluded all but the very minimum of anecdotal material. I owe them a debt that is impossible to repay, not least because they entrusted me with the public image of the club or organisation they are deeply committed to.

I have tried hard on their behalf to be accurate and positive. I hope I have succeeded.

A big debt is owed to *Cycling* newspaper and I am happy to acknowledge it, not least because of the pleasure the newspaper has given me over the years, but specifically for permission to quote. Acknowledgement is given, with appropriate references, in the text. Research into such a vast subject, and the ability to provide a bibliography, would not have been possible without access to books – Leicestershire Libraries were extremely helpful, providing me with a copy of every cycling book in stock. Heffers bookshops, Cambridge, accorded me time and courtesy whilst using their facilities, and I am very grateful. Others who gave unstintingly of their time and energy are mentioned in the Acknowledgements, with my gratitude.

Despite the considerable help given to me, any misconceptions or mistakes that remain are totally my own responsibility. One problem, of course, with such a publication is that information can quickly be out of date. I hope that any mistakes or necessary alterations will be brought to my attention so that, should the book be popular enough to require a second edition, it can be corrected and brought up to date.

One last plea: forgive my use of 'he', 'him', etc., when it should properly – but laboriously – be 'he/she', 'him/her', etc.

Philip Ennis
Rutland
June 1983

ACKNOWLEDGEMENTS

Colin Brierly – CTC Devon DA; Gordon R. Stephen – ACHE; R. J. Richards – BCCA; Lieut K. H. Waller – RN & RMCA; Eric Tremaine; Mrs D. Tuffnell – TA; B. Chilcott – BCF; Pat Constance – AC & LC; Terry Smith; Wally Happy – SWOMA; Timothy C. Neal; Andy Ingram; Trevor Taylor; Bruce Thomas, Sid Ferris, Sam Lee – Veges C & AC; Geoff Wiles – UK-BMX; Dudley Roberts – RTTC; Dennis Clayton – Tyne RC; Arthur A. Butcher – CTC SW London DA (Wayfarers); Mrs Bridgett Ellis – NAVCC; Ken McDonald – Glade CC; H. G. Robson – RSF; H. W. Pink – South Eastern RC; John Nicholas – AUK; G. W. Hunton – RRA; Newy Nottingham, Mrs Chris Watts – WRRA; Howard N. Boyd – RoSPA; Douglas Smith – CTC Falkirk & C Scotland DA; John Haigh – OCD; Sid Haywood – VTTA; R. K. Londragan – SCU; Michael E. Ware – National Motor Museum, Beaulieu; Roy Knight – Leicestershire Libraries; Mrs J. Foster – BAGB; Peter Hopkins – ESCA; Cycle Speedway Council; Malcolm Smith – London St Christophers CCC; John A. Wood – Clifton CC; John Roxburgh – CTC Glasgow DA; T. M. McNamara – BCCS; Don Mathew – FoE; Ron Johnson; John Else; David Watson – Heffers; John Allen – CTC Leicestershire DA; Joe Summerlin – 24-hour Fellowship; Bernard and Ethel Thompson; Alan Leng – CTC.

1
CLUBS AND ORGANISATIONS

The criteria applied in compiling this chapter have been simple: to describe the opportunities available to cyclists provided by cycling clubs and organisations, and to show how individuals can take advantage of them.

All of the major clubs and organisations are described, and many smaller specialist clubs. As will be seen later, some national bodies are for affiliated clubs only; others include private members or are composed entirely of individual subscribers.

Some of the smaller organisations are exclusive (for example, a cycling club for doctors) or set standards which make the club exclusive (for instance, the author will never be eligible to join the 300,000 Club which requires documentary evidence that would-be members have cycled 300,000+ miles; the author has logged nearly 120,000 in the last twenty years, but for many years did not keep a record of miles ridden!).

In addition to the facts given below, the facilities provided by the various cycling clubs are mentioned at appropriate points elsewhere in the book.

The Cyclists' Touring Club (CTC)
Cotterell House, 69 Meadrow, Godalming, Surrey GU7 3HS

This is the oldest established cycling organisation in existence. Founded at Harrogate on 5 August 1878 by

Stanley Cotterell, it was known as the Bicycle Touring Club, adopting its present title in 1883. Its primary object has always been: 'to promote, assist and protect the use of bicycles, tricycles and other similar vehicles on the public roads and public rights of way'.

CTC policy is decided and developed by its National Council, an elected body of honorary officials. Any CTC member is eligible for election to the Council.

The success and strength of the Club resides in its District Associations (DAs), some fifty-five in all, covering all parts of England, Wales and Northern Ireland, much of Scotland and parts of Eire. The District Associations are based on cities, counties or parts of counties, or larger geographical areas depending upon population. The DAs themselves consist of sections, which may be local cycling clubs affiliated to the CTC or groups of cyclists in towns or areas who organise cycling activities on an autonomous but cooperative basis within the DA.

All members of the CTC are automatically listed as members of the District Association where they live. On their behalf the DA committee arranges a variety of cycling and social events.

Cyclists may participate or contribute at various levels within their DA. They may simply join the rides organised regularly by the DA or sections; they may act as officials on DA and/or section committees; they may lead organised rides on a rota basis; they may offer their services at special events (such as officiating on standard rides, helping to organise annual family gatherings, etc.). The membership framework, however, is deliberately loose and no pressure is put on any member to take part in organised activities. Indeed, there are CTC members who take little or no part in DA events (for all sorts of reasons), riding alone or with their families and finding benefits from CTC membership through the Club's other provisions.

District Association activities

These are best exemplified by quoting from actual DA programmes in various parts of Britain.

Devon District Association

Secretary: Colin Brierly, 24 Great Headland Crescent, Paignton, Devon

The DA, which recently celebrated its fiftieth anniversary, has the distinction that one of its members is President of the CTC. This is Ivy Thorp, who with her husband Gordon, takes an active part in 'grass roots' organisation in the DA.

The DA has four sections: Torbay, Exeter 'A' (Aways), Exeter 'B' (The Bee's Knees), and Plymouth (The Sound). The hub of the social scene is the Exeter clubroom, with occasional get-togethers at Torbay. Members take part in regular rides, hostel weekends, popular 'coffee-pot' runs, photographic competitions, carol singing, parties . . .

The sections ride to such picturesque destinations as Bickleigh Castle, Budleigh Salterton and Chudleigh Chuckles, and stop for refreshments at the Southern Cross Cafe, the Queen of Hearts Cafe, the Black Cat Cafe . . .

Details of all the DA's rides and activities are published bimonthly in *The Highwayman*, a lively publication full of interest and humour. Recent articles have varied from a report by a twelve year old of his sponsored ride for charity, the Torbay Juniors' tour to South Wales and a member's eleven-day 'Irish Jaunt', to a humorous piece which began: 'As I remember, it all started because of this girl.'

Glasgow District Association
*Secretary: John Roxburgh, 9 Wynyard Green,
East Kilbride, Glasgow*

This DA has been in existence for more than eighty years. It has a regular programme of Sunday rides, with parallel rides for Easyriders which average 40–50 miles. A separate 'Vetruns' section has regular monthly rides which favour the Renfrewshire Lanes.

In the east of the city is the Eagle Road club, a racing section open to CTC members only and providing a full programme of events (from March–September) – time trials, track, road races and a hill climb.

The DA regularly uses Scottish youth hostels, organised groups going, for example, to the far north and the Isle of Skye, but it does have its own 'ledi hut', at Stank, near Strathyre, which provides cheap but excellent accommodation. It publishes an annual handbook and has clubroom facilities (darts, table tennis, slide and film shows, etc.) in Glasgow and at Bailleston (Garrowhill section).

Their eightieth anniversary celebrations included an 80-mile sponsored ride which raised £630 to buy exercise bikes (what else?!) for the physiotherapy department of the Victoria Infirmary.

The Falkirk and Central Scotland District Association
*Secretary: Douglas Smith, 28 Napier Place, Bainsford,
Falkirk*

This DA started life in 1952 as a section of the Glasgow DA. Its steady progress over the years culminated in its organising the CTC's BCTC final in 1981, and the CTC Dinner and Prize Presentation in the same year.

In addition to its year-round runs, when there are one or more 'drum up' points en route to enable slower riders to catch up, the DA puts on a full programme of activities. These include a weekly club night, with film shows once a month, given by club members, the Falkirk Camera Club, and members of Glasgow, Fife and Lothians DAs.

Competitions held include: photographic, free-wheel, hill climb, speed judging and treasure hunts. In early June, a sports day is held at Blackness, and they join in Glasgow DA's Kinlochard Social which incorporates a weekend at Loch Ard hostel.

The highlight of the year is the dinner and prize presentation.

Leicestershire District Association
Secretary: John Allen, 223 Main Street,
Stanton-under-Bardon, Coalville

This large and thriving DA has several sections (Charnwood, City, Kibworth, Loiterers & Photographic, Loughborough and Lutterworth) which together provide an enormous range of activities (including non-cycling events such as rambling, swimming and football!).

Organised rides go to all points of the compass, speeds and distances being varied to accommodate the abilities of the riders. Some sections are particularly strong in family rides.

Special events are legion – standard rides, BCTC heats, cycle rallies, free-wheel and map-reading competitions – with popular events including Skegness-and-back, the Mince Pie run, etc. Special social events include the annual carol service, New Year party and slide show.

The DA magazine is *Cycle Chat*, published quarterly. The DA has a strong tradition in the field of cyclists' rights, takes part fully in CTC national and international events, and has close links with county cycle-racing clubs, being a founder-member of the Leicestershire Cyclists' Association (LCA). The DA is always a strong contender for the CTC's Carter-Ruck trophy, awarded to the DA recruiting most members in the year, winning the trophy in 1979.

On the competitive side, the DA organises standard rides (for example 100 miles in six hours), awarding medals at gold, silver and bronze levels, the rides also contributing to the LCA Tourist BAR (Best All-Rounder).

And an untypical *section*:

South West London DA – Midweek Wayfarers Wednesday Section
Secretary: Arthur A. Butcher, 196 Elm Road, New Malden, Surrey KT3 3HT ☎ 01-942 7479

This section, formed in 1980, comprises 90 per cent senior citizens, oldest seventy-six years. It provides a midweek ride for retired cyclists in south-west London and has proved so attractive that its numbers include schoolchildren, when on holiday, and also shift workers.

They meet at 9.45 a.m. at the Queen Victoria, North Cheam, for a variety of rides in counties from Kent to Berkshire, some train-assisted to places such as Horsham, Guildford, Dorking and Petersfield. The all-day runs average 50 miles. A keen leader of runs is the indomitable 'Chater' Willis, and the strength of the section is illustrated by the fact that twelve runs in April/May 1983 had twelve different leaders. (Psst! Nearly all runs have cake-shop stops.)

Members also attend events further afield, including the CTC's Birthday Rides, and organise mini-tours of up to four days at youth hostels.

Annual Report 1981 – Extract
'It is generally agreed amongst members that their

fitness and well-being has improved over the last year due it is felt to regular cycling and the happy atmosphere engendered by the fellowship . . .'

Apart from the cycling activities described above, the CTC member has access to the following benefits:

1. *A handbook* (on joining). This is issued each year. Its chief benefit is in listing addresses and giving details of caterers, repairers, etc., in towns and villages throughout Britain. The lists are built over the years on members' recommendations and can be relied upon to provide a sound and sympathetic service.
2. *Cycletouring* magazine, issued bimonthly free to members. It contains articles, trade news and all types of cycling information.
3. Free *third party insurance* cover and *legal aid* in fighting for compensation for injury sustained while cycling.
4. *Information* by way of:
   (a) leaflets on all aspects of cycle touring in Britain and abroad – details in the handbook.
   (b) Local information officers in many localities who offer their knowledge of the area to cyclists visiting or passing through – names and addresses are listed in the handbook.

British Cycling Federation (BCF)
Secretary: Mr L. Unwin, 16 Upper Woburn Place, London WC1

The BCF was originally inaugurated in 1878 as the Bicycle Union, but in 1884 became the National Cyclists Union (NCU), a name it retained until 1959 when it amalgamated with the British League of Racing Cyclists (BLRC). It controls amateur and professional riding in connection with road racing, circuit racing and track events, and, as such, is the National Cycling Body representing Great Britain for all cycle sport.

The activities of the BCF are controlled through divisional delegates attending National Council who define the broad policy and elect members to the Finance & Management Committee and Racing Committee, to supervise the running and day-to-day business of the Federation.

The BCF promoted and organised the 1982 World Cycling Championships (track events at Leicester's Saffron Lane, and the Road Racing Championships at Goodwood, Sussex).

Its benefits to members include: insurance claims of up to £500,000 by third parties, the BCF handling the matter on the member's behalf; free legal aid should a member have an accident for which someone else is responsible; touring facilities, including the planning of a cycling holiday at home or abroad.

Road Time Trials Council (RTTC)
National Secretary: Mr D. E. Roberts, 'Dallacre',
Mill Road, Yarwell, Peterborough PE8 6PS

The purpose of the Council (founded 1922 as The Road Racing Council) is to control unpaced cycling time trials on public roads in England and Wales. This sounds simple; it is anything but simple. The number of permutations of distances, machines and riders is considerable. Thus every distance between 10 miles and 24 hours is possible, for bicycle, tandem, tricycle and tandem tricycle, for professionals, amateurs, men, women, teams, juveniles and juniors.

In any one year, some 2,000 open events will be staged by the 840 or so affiliated clubs and associations, with as many more club events.

Clubs will use every ounce of ingenuity in devising variations on the time trial theme. Several clubs take the opportunity of civic festivals to stage time trials near to town centres. Adorior RC puts on a Circuit of Kinder; Nelson Wheelers, a Circuit of the Dales. It might be expected that Buxton CC would organise a mountain time trial, but imagine the audacity of Spalding CC in staging a Hilly event!

The Council organises National Championships at various distances for men, women, teams, juveniles and juniors, and among the many fine trophies available for competition, is the George Herbert Stancer (GHS) Memorial for the 10-mile Juvenile/School Team Championship.

The British Best All-Rounder (BBAR) competition is for men, women and teams. The trophy for the men's BBAR is a cup known as the 'Lincoln Trophy', won outright by Herbert Synger in 1888. The women's cup was presented by Mrs Ethel Brambleby to crown a competition which has been won, for twenty-four consecutive years to 1982, by the 'queen' of cycling, the incredible Mrs Beryl Burton, OBE.

Records set under time trial conditions are known as 'competition records' and must not be confused with the 'non-competitive' records of the RRA (qv).

Road Records Association (RRA)

Honorary Secretary: Mr G. W. Hunton, 20 Ley Road, Farnborough, Hampshire GU14 8EB

This prestigious and long-standing association was founded in 1888 'to verify and certify the genuineness of claims to best performances on record accomplished by male cyclists on the road'.

From the beginning it has set the highest standards of accuracy in authenticating records. Of the Association's seventy-nine rules no fewer than forty-six relate directly to a record-breaking attempt. As part of its rigorous check on record attempts, the Association can call on the services of thirty official timekeepers, ninety-three official observers and twenty-five official course measurers, plus a large number of checkers throughout England, Wales and Scotland.

The following records on bicycle, tricycle, tandem bicycle and tandem tricycle are recognised by the Association:

    25 miles
    50 miles
    100 miles
    1,000 miles
    12 hours
    24 hours
    Land's End to John o'Groats (End to End)
    Land's End to London
    London to York
    York to Edinburgh
    London to Liverpool
    Liverpool to Edinburgh
    London to Edinburgh
    London to Bath and back
    London to Brighton and back
    London to Portsmouth and back
    London to Pembroke
    London to Cardiff
    London to Birmingham

The RRA rules make fascinating reading:
(72) 'Where the BBC Sound Radio Time Signal is

used for the watch check, the sixth pip shall be the starting point.'
(37) 'In any attempt on record the rider . . . when dismounted shall wheel or carry his . . . machine without assistance . . .'

If you want to break the London to Cardiff record, held by Phil Griffiths (1971) with a time of 5 hours 54 minutes 14 seconds, you will be required to start or finish 'opposite the stone marking the site of Tyburn Tree, situated on a traffic island at the junction of Edgware and Bayswater roads at Marble Arch . . .'
Membership of the Association is for:
(a) affiliated cycle clubs,
(b) private members.
In 1982, 103 clubs were affiliated to the RRA, two of which – Anfield BC and North Road CC – are founder members.

Anyone wishing to attempt records should seek help and advice from those experienced in organising such attempts, and the benefits that are available, through joining one of the clubs affiliated to the RRA. A pamphlet giving detailed information on record attempts can be obtained from the RRA. Anyone interested in acting as an official or checker should also contact the Association.

Aspiring record breakers should read Bernard Thompson's article: 'Records Ripe for Breaking' (*Cycling*, 2 February 1980), in which he states persuasively: '. . . few of the (now 76) records in the RRA Handbook are unapproachable by any of the current top time triallists or roadmen'. This must be true when one considers that some records have stood for over twenty years and one – The Twelve-hour bicycle (276½ miles) – since 1939.

Women's Road Records Association (WRRA)

Secretary: Mr N. G. Nottingham, 36 Hill View Gardens, Kingsbury, London NW9 0TE

This parallel organisation to the RRA was formed in 1934 to verify and certify claims to records by female cyclists. There are forty-three records available for breaking, not all identical to the RRA's (for example: 100 kilometres (62 miles); London to Oxford and back; Edinburgh to Glasgow and back).

It is interesting to note that four records (100 kilometres/62 miles tandem; 12 hours tricycle; 24 hours tandem and tricycle) have never been set – a great opportunity existing for someone brave. Long-standing records ready for breaking include the 50 miles bicycle record (1 hour 59 minutes 14 seconds) which has stood since 1940.

The ladies really do things properly: when the 1,000 miles record was broken in 1974 the course was cleverly scheduled around the record-breaker's home city, so that she could get home regularly for a 'wash and brush up'.

Some thirty clubs/associations are affiliated to the WRRA, many of whose officers are past and present record holders.

The secretary is Mr ('I am a Mister') Newy Nottingham – correspondents please note. Members receive an annual handbook, plus a twice-yearly newsletter.

Scottish Cyclists' Union (SCU)

Secretary: Mr R. K. Londragan, 89 Ashley Road, Aberdeen AB1 6RL

Founded in 1889, the SCU's main object is to govern and encourage all aspects of cycle sport in Scotland.

For ease of administration the country is divided into eight geographical centres. Members of the SCU belong to cycling clubs, within each centre, affiliated to the Union.

Each centre has its own (honorary) officers, clubs, commissaires (senior official at an event), time-keepers, recorders and coaches, who are responsible under the authority of the Union for all time trials, road and track races.

Members are kept informed by the circulation of regular bulletins and the annual handbook.

Because the Union is organised with professional skill, concessions are always made to help the very youngest and most inexperienced to join the racing ranks. So: 'Competitors must wear their own club's registered colours' (Denny RC, Falkirk, is: yellow with one 3-inch black hoop, one 3-inch white and one 3-inch red hoop and one in piping!) 'or black'.

The Union organises a full range of National Championship races and BAR competitions for men/women, schoolboys/girls, juniors, and veterans. Many of the competitions carry prestigious trophies. For example, the Junior BAR (sixteen–eighteen year olds) carries the Raleigh Trophy for the fastest combined speed over distances of 25 and 50 miles. Is there a junior around who can beat S. McCaw's (1980) speed of 25.572 mph?

Northern Ireland Cycling Federation (NICF)
Secretary: Mr J. Henry, 20 Thornleigh Gardens, Bangor, Co. Down

This organisation, similar to the BCF (England and Wales) and SCU (Scotland) administers cycle racing in the Republic.

British Cyclo-Cross Association (BCCA)

General Secretary: Mr R. J. Richards, 8 Bellam Road,
Hampton Magna, nr Warwick

The BCCA includes in its constitution the aims: 'to control cyclo-cross in England and Wales . . . and to encourage cyclo-cross as training for cycle racing'. This latter aim is important. Cyclo-cross takes place in the 'off' season September to February, and enables racing cyclists to keep fit during winter. For most cyclo-cross enthusiasts, however, it is an end in itself, and they use time trials and road races to keep fit *for* the winter.

The Association was formed in 1954 and now consists of some 300 affiliated clubs. Prior to 1954 there were only six established races in the country, including the well-known Walsall Cyclists v. Harriers, dating back to 1921.

Cyclo-cross is a competitive cross-country cycle race. The course is usually 1–2 miles long, several circuits of the course giving the race a length of 10–15 miles (proportionately less for juniors and schoolboys), which takes 60–75 minutes to cover. It is a rugged sport, designed to be so. The Association recommends: 'Unrideable stretches should be short but rough and the use of terrain calling for skilled machine handling and balance encouraged,' and 'that all riders have an anti-tetanus inoculation prior to the season'.

Cyclo-cross riders will battle with snow and ice, clinging mud, log-filled streams and treacherous slopes, but the toughest test on the calendar must be the 50-kilometre (31-mile) Three Peaks event, to which the 'Bradford RCC invite entries from fit and well-prepared riders for their classic race over the three peaks of Whernside, Ingleborough and Pen-y-ghent'.

The BCCA organises National Championship events with supporting categories for veterans, juniors and schoolboys, and a season-long Trophy League which (with its precursor, the Viking Trophy) has been won by the 'greats' in cyclo-cross – Stallard, Mernickle, Atkins, Dodd and Wreghitt.

Vegetarian Cycling & Athletic Club (VC & AC)

Secretary: Bruce Thomas, 2 Lookers Park Lane, Hemel Hempstead, Hertfordshire

This venerable organisation began as long ago as 1887. The Club had forty-eight members when seventeen cyclists set off for the first ride of 1888 'from Clapham . . . to Epsom, where fruit was partaken of at Schulks' Coffee Tavern. The hostess, . . . provided the usual coffee and tea, cakes and eggs, marmalade, etc. . . .'.

The Club's close links with both cycling and athletics are illustrated by the fact that Sam Lee, the athletics secretary, has been a member for fifty years, including twenty-eight years of cycle racing.

The Club's early excursions into cycle touring developed rapidly into competitive cycling (Club motto: 'Feed well, speed well') with remarkable results.

For example, G. B. Olley twice broke the Land's End to John o'Groats record (1905 and 1908), his 3 days 5 hours 20 minutes being further reduced by the great Syd Ferris (1937) to 2 days 6 hours 33 minutes and by Dave Keeler (1958) to 2 days 3 hours 9 minutes. Club members and Club teams have set standards and achieved performances unrivalled by any club in Britain, and the VC and AC is as alive and active as ever it was.

It has branches throughout Britain, publishes an

annual handbook and a quarterly magazine. Sometime, somehow, someone will publish a full history of this astonishing 'green triangle' club, building on the delightful duplicated *'History of the Veges' – The story of a Club and a Cause (1888–1973)*, by A. Dobson.

Veterans' Time Trials Association (VTTA)

Secretary: Mr S. E. Haywood, 137 Glenwood Avenue, Westcliff-on-Sea, Essex

The VTTA has grown from forty at the inaugural meeting at High Barnet in 1943 to well over four thousand members in some fifteen groups covering England, Scotland and Wales.

Each group runs its own time trials, being affiliated to the RTTC, and there are national Championships at all distances from 10 miles to 24 hours. Anyone over forty years old may join the Association, all of whose events are open to over-forties, whether members or not. Only members, however, are eligible for Championship awards.

Veterans' events are run with the principal award going to the fastest *on standard*. The standard tables consist of set times for each distance at each age. For example, Arthur Wilkins (Verulam CC) was allowed 1 hour 26 minutes 56 seconds for a 25-mile time trial but the seventy-seven year old rode a magnificent 1–9–21 to take the top award from younger faster veterans.

Prior to the formation of the VTTA, the RTTC had resisted a 12-hour event for veterans, expressing grave fears 'that the North Road would be strewn with elderly gentlemen in all stages of distress, doctors and ambulances'. In the event an over sixty year old cycled 174½ miles. The current record of an eighty year old (J. A. Shuter, 1967) is 161.44 miles.

Lady veterans were welcomed into membership in 1971.

Each group has its own social calendar. At national level, the main event is the Easter Rally at Warwick, which includes the AGM, lunch and Championship awards presentation. An annual handbook, bimonthly *Veteran*, and group newsletters keep the members informed.

Rough Stuff Fellowship (RSF)

Secretary: Fred E. Goatcher, 65 Stoneleigh Avenue, Worcester Park, Surrey KT4 8XY

The Rough Stuff Fellowship (formed 1955) is for: 'cyclists who love byways and tracks'. The Fellowship brings together like-minded enthusiasts to explore the drovers' roads, green lanes, bridleways and mountain tracks which provide an enormous range of touring opportunities.

Membership is open to all cyclists over fourteen who can declare a genuine interest in rough stuff riding. The BSF is organised into area groups, for example Scotland's 'Vagabond Group', which has such mottoes as: Use out-of-date map for exciting rough-stuff! The BSF holds an annual Easter Meet (and AGM) always at a different venue. Its bimonthly *Rough-Stuff Journal* is issued to each member.

But, be warned, the Journal is notorious for turning armchair travellers into real enthusiasts, and one could easily end up, as one member did, rescuing a sheep which had been trapped in a hedge for a week – which leads to a serious point: do not go rough stuffing alone. Join the RSF and your rough-stuff fellows are more than companions; they know a thing or two about survival and how to cope with emergencies.

Tricycle Association (TA)

National Secretary: Mrs D. Tuffnell, 92 Graham Gardens,
Luton, Bedfordshire LU3 1NQ

The TA was founded in 1928 following an informal
'natter-and-noggin' in the 'Crown', Theale, by tricyclists, including Alec Glass, who had taken part in a
Western Roads '50'.

The first official ride, to the Anchor Inn at Ripley,
involved fourteen tricyclists whose 'fast riding and
demon cornering' led to at least two sets of wheels
interlocking with disastrous results. The TA grew and
flourished, meets and races continuing through the
War when events sometimes occurred under skies full
of planes dog-fighting and rides home were in pitch
darkness, lit only by flames from the blitz and anti-
aircraft tracer shells.

The Association is organised under eight regions to
which members belong, each region holding its own
racing, touring and social programme. In addition,
there are three National time trials each year – the
Bruce Kingsford Memorial '50', the Stan Spelling
'25', the competition for the Tricycle Trophy in rota-
tion at 50, 100 miles, 12 and 24 hours – and a **BBAR**
competition.

The Women's TA, formed in 1954, came under the
TA umbrella in 1978.

A quarterly Gazette is circulated to keep members
informed of all TA activities, and an up-dated history
was due to be published in 1983. Honours gained by
tricyclists and 'broad-gauge' (tandem tricycle) riders
over the years are legion, but mention must be made
of a recent dramatic achievement – Eric Tremaine's
1982 record for the End to End.

Audax United Kingdom (AUK)
Secretary: John Nicholas, 188 Runcorn Road, Moore,
Warrington WA4 6SY

Audax (Latin: bold) began in Italy in 1897, contestants having to use their own muscle power to cover a specified distance between dawn and dusk (14 hours). For cyclists the distance was 200 kilometres/124 miles.

Internationally the most prestigious offspring of the idea is the quadrennial Paris–Brest–Paris (PBP) Randonneur, where a distance of 1,206 kilometres (750 miles) has to be completed inside 90 hours, successful riders being awarded a Brevet PBP. To qualify for entry to the PBP several lesser events have to be completed.

AUK was formed to establish qualifying Randonnées in Britain for the PBP, and in 1976 the first 600-kilometre (373-mile) Windsor–Chester–Windsor (WCW) was organised. Since the first ride, Randonnées have become extremely popular.

Randonnées are not races. Specified distances are covered in specified times (for example, 300 kilometres/186 miles in 20 hours (maximum) or 10 hours (minimum); 1,200 kilometres (746 miles) in 90 hours or 40 hours). In some events each entrant states the conditions of his ride and then tries to match his ambition to reality. Advertised control points along the route, where brevet cards are stamped, and a secret control, ensure both steady progress towards and the essential confirmation of success.

Apart from the brevet card, which can be kept as a souvenir, a date pendant and/or medallion of success are available at nominal cost.

The Brevet-Populaire (100 kilometres/62 miles) is a very short ride, one of which was organised recently by the South Yorkshire & North Derbyshire DA/CTC and completed successfully by an eight year old and an eighty year old. (Petit-Brevet (50 kilometres/31 miles) is available for novices, families, etc.).

Membership of AUK is open to *any* cyclist 'who is imbued with the spirit of long distance cycling and who is a person of goodwill'. Nominal entry fees admit members and non-members to events (but less for members!).

L'Ordre des Cols Durs (OCD)
Secretary: Tim Neal, 14 Springfield Avenue, Southbourne, Bournemouth, Dorset

The English-speaking group of this French 'pass-storming' organisation began in the mid 1960s. The idea is to scale mountain passes or high hills (over 300 metres) by road or rough-stuff, keeping a tally of the height. Aggregate claims of over 50,000 metres can be sent each year to OCD to achieve initial membership.

Later stages are:	Officer	100,000 metres
	Commander	200,000 metres
	Honourable	500,000 metres
	Venerable	1,000,000 metres

How much cycling does 50,000 metres represent? A good total for a week's touring in the Alps would amass half that figure, and rather less than half could be claimed by riders in the 1982 Tour de France.

The British OCD has a varied membership. The youngest to qualify did so when only fourteen years old. Members rarely go abroad to tackle high mountains. Indeed, two of the three largest totals came from within the United Kingdom. By 1982 five members had passed 300,000 metres; the first British member to reach 1,000,000 metres, and thus qualify for membership of the French OCD, is Keith Barker, editor of *Cycloclimbing*.

English-speaking cyclists aspiring to membership

will be relieved to know that the French Rule 8 is optional: 'Each candidate . . . should write a four-line rhyme in honour of mountain cycling . . . in French.'

The OCD in Britain publishes a magazine, *Cyclo-climbing*, three times a year.

National Association of Veteran Cycle Clubs (NAVCC)
Secretary: Mrs Bridgett Ellis, 80 Garnsgate Road,
Long Sutton, Spalding, Lincolnshire

The NAVCC comprises seven Veteran Cycle Clubs:
    The Benson Veteran Cycle Club
    Belton House Museum Veteran Cycle Club
    The Boston Veteran Bicycle Club
    Bygone Bykes, Yorkshire Club
    Desford Lane (Leicester) Pedallers' Veteran Cycle Club
    The Long Sutton & District Veteran Cycle Club
    The Peterborough Vintage Cycle Club
The Association's aims are to 'restore, preserve and ride the old cycles with dignity . . . .'. An annual rally is held in a different county each year. The individual clubs attend rallies, carnivals, galas, etc., nearly always in aid of charity, the riders invariably wearing period dress. In recent years the clubs have attended such noble venues as Windsor Castle, Glamis Castle and Sandringham – dignity indeed.

The NAVCC's members have a magnificent selection of cycles: high ordinaries (which the 'hoi polloi' call penny-farthings), solid-tyred tricycles, bone-shakers, solid-tyred safety cycles of many shapes and sizes, and early pneumatic tyres.

(NB Veteran cycles are those pre-1914; vintage cycles are around or more than fifty years old. Does yours qualify?)

English Schools Cycling Association (ESCA)

General Secretary: Mr P. A. W. Dixon,
6 Malmers Well Road, High Wycombe, Buckinghamshire
HP13 6PD ☎ 0494 446857

ESCA was formed in 1967 to encourage cycling as a school activity, hoping thereby to produce more and better cyclists at all types of cycling sport and recreation.

Membership is open to all children, mostly of secondary school age, and school membership is possible via interested teachers. Some schools have cycling (for example cyclo-cross) on the curriculum, others organise cycle tours. ESCA feeds this interest by organising a programme of activities at local and national level, such as cyclo-cross and circuit races, and time trials. Touring facilities also exist and members can qualify for awards at bronze, silver and gold level for racing, standard rides and hostelling.

Perhaps the most successful of ESCA's events is the annual Butlin's International, involving the top riders in three days of competitive racing.

ESCA has recently introduced 'The Cycling Teaching Certificate' in conjunction with the BCCS (qv), suitable for teachers, youth club leaders, etc., who wish to introduce cycling to the curriculum.

Royal Navy & Royal Marines Cycling Association (RN & RM CA)

General Secretary: Lieutenant K. H. Waller, RN,
HMS Nelson, Portsmouth, Hampshire

The Association was formed in 1950 following the success of the Portsmouth Command Club, its two immediate aims being:

'to secure Admiralty recognition of cycling as an official sport, and to persuade Commanding Officers of HM Ships to allow cyclists to stow their machines on board and to proceed ashore in cycling rig.'

These were soon achieved, and cycling quickly became an official sport with a full programme of service and inter-service championships. Touring and racing cycles are now a common sight on board ship and members have ridden in almost all parts of the world.

Full membership of the RN & RM CA is open to all serving personnel of the RN, RM and WRNS.

The Association seeks to encourage the formation of cycling clubs in all ships and establishments of the Navy at home and abroad, and assists and advises clubs on all aspects of cycle racing, touring, hostelling and expeditions. It awards certificates for beating standard times or distances at 10, 25, 30, 50, 100 miles and 12 and 24 hours; and trophies and RN Cycling Colours for exceptional achievements.

Such an Association faces extraordinary difficulties, as for example when 'promoters of the 30-mile time trial and the Lee Circuit races were given "pierhead jumps"', i.e., were suddenly posted elsewhere!

It keeps its members informed by a monthly newsletter and makes light of its problems, as instanced in the racing secretary's report for 1982: 'The Argentine government failed to appreciate the importance of the early season races and chose the week of the first Inter-Service events to invade the Falklands'.

United Kingdom Bicycle Motocross Association (UKBMX)

National Director: Mr G. Wiles, 47 Cuxton Road, Strood, Kent ME2 2BU

BMX originated in California in the early 1970s and UKBMX was established in 1980. The sport consists of races on light, strong 20-inch-wheel cycles around a short closed circuit of between 200 and 400 metres. The age of the contestants varies from five years to over twenty. Each participant rides in a group according to his age on 1 January and stays in that group for the whole year.

The race: six or eight riders take part in each heat of one complete circuit (called a moto); each rider has three motos, and points are given according to position; the riders with the lowest points then go on to qualify in quarterfinals, semifinals and finals.

The circuit: this can be varied to include jumps, turns and other obstacles to add excitement; safety is paramount; riders *must* wear full protective clothing – long trousers, helmets, and long-sleeved jerseys. Full insurance cover is provided for members whenever riding a bicycle.

Events are organised within regions (eleven in all) and temporary membership *on the day* enables new riders immediate access to the sport.

The Cycle Speedway Council (CSC)

Central Office: 9 Meadow Close, Hethersett, Norwich, Norfolk

The CSC was founded in 1971 to unify all cycle speedway organisations, and to develop national competitions. About ninety affiliated clubs (over 200 teams) compete in five major and thirteen minor leagues in England, Scotland and Wales.

The oval tracks vary in length from 70 to 100 metres, are usually shale surfaced, and banked at the 'bends'. Four riders race heats of four laps, anticlockwise. The bikes are basic, being designed with quick acceleration, steep banking and safety in mind. Wheels are standard $26 \times 1\frac{3}{8}$ inch with gripster tyres; pedals are rubber; there are no gears, just a freewheel of say 32:18; and no brakes.

Spectators are important to the sport and most tracks provide seating, comprehensive programmes, refreshments, a public address system, etc.

The blue riband of the sport is the annual British Championship. Preliminary 'knockout' rounds culminate in the top sixty-four riders competing over a bank holiday weekend for the title British Cycle Speedway Champion. There are also categories for Youth (Under-21), Junior (Under-18) and Schoolboy (Under-15) Champions.

Association of Cycle and Lightweight Campers (AC & LC)

Honorary Secretary: Mr P. H. Constance,
c/o The Camping Club of Great Britain & Ireland Ltd,
11 Lower Grosvenor Place, London SW1W 0EY

Formed under the title 'Association of Cycle Campers' in 1901, the AC & LC is now a section of the Camping Club of Great Britain. Members of the Association are first members of the Club, paying a small additional subscription to obtain the benefits of the specialist section.

Members receive a quarterly 'bulletin', post free, and other benefits, including insurance, Club monthly magazine and the members' handbook and sites guide. The Club owns or manages over sixty sites and the guide lists many more which are privately or commercially owned, large and small.

The Association is run entirely by volunteers – honorary elected officials – and cannot provide a free information service on specific sites, routes, etc. It can, however, given sufficient time, elicit from within its membership first-hand experience and advice on all aspects of lightweight cycle camping. It is particularly well-placed to advise on suitable kit, including tents, and keeps abreast of all the latest developments at home and abroad. (Enquiries should always be accompanied by a stamped addressed envelope.)

The Association arranges many small 'local meets', since most lightweight campers tend to avoid large gatherings, but it holds an Easter rally and the September AGM rally on a large scale. Individual members, or families, may prefer to camp alone, but still have the benefits and support of the Association.

British Cycling Coaching Scheme (BCCS)

Coaching Administrator: Mr T. M. McNamara,
24 Ascot Road, Kippax, Leeds LS25 7HT

The BCCS is sponsored jointly by the BCF and RTTC. It has several objects, but chiefly to be responsible for the training and examination of coaches, these in turn to raise the standard of cycle riding/racing to its highest level.

The grades of coach are: assistant (student), club, regional and senior. Coaches of all grades begin as students, completing a training course, examinations and practical assignments. The student syllabus is in five modules with a question paper at the end of each. Every aspect of the cycle and its uses is covered, plus training, diet, first aid and physiology, etc. Two years are allowed in which to complete the course, a certificate and badge being awarded.

A regional coach will have completed a rigorous reading programme with set questions, and an intensive study of, for example, first aid.

One of the coach's jobs is to 'help the development of the (young) rider into becoming a fit, healthy, happy and worthy member of society, as well as a successful racing cyclist'. This sensible attitude pervades the readable modules put out for study.

The BCCS also awards (jointly with ESCA) a Cycling Training Certificate suitable for teachers, youth leaders, etc., enabling them to introduce cycling as a school or extra-curricular activity. The syllabus covers cycling basics, safety, equipment, cycling organisations, competitions and awards, etc. Some twenty hours of study are required, as are written and practical examinations, and (here's the Parthian dart!) a standard ride of 15 miles.

The Bicycle Association of Great Britain (BA) (and British Cycling Bureau (BCB))
Registered Office: Starley House, Eaton Road, Coventry CV1 2FH

The BA is a trade association for the bicycle industry, representing bicycle, accessories and components manufacturers. It refers to itself as: 'the voice of the industry', being contacted by Government departments concerning legislation, etc. It campaigns vigorously for the maintenance of national and international standards for bicycles. The association uses its funds, levied from members, for a variety of promotional activities, for example: to persuade the public to buy reputable bicycles through reputable outlets, making the public aware of the dangers of cheap and inferior quality machines.

The BCB is a (currently) low-key part of the association.

Association of Cycle Traders (ACT)
31A High Street, Tunbridge Wells, Kent TN1 1XN
☎ 0892 26081

The Association – whose roots go back to 1920 – acts as an advice office for cycle dealers. It can provide information on setting up and running cycle shops and cycle hire facilities, including advice on income tax and VAT, how to cope with part exchange and guarantees, etc. Its aim is to help the dealer provide a first class pre-sales and after-sales service to customers. It also organises joint publicity between dealers and manufacturers to minimise costs and thus benefit both them and the customers.

Cycling Clubs

Space does not permit a description of the facilities provided by the many hundreds of cycle clubs. Five clubs are included here, with just a brief look at some of their facilities to give an idea of the flavour of club life.

South-Eastern Road Club (SERC)
General Secretary: Mrs S. H. Clinch,
78 Limpsfield Avenue, Thornton Heath, Surrey CR4 6BF

This is a club (founded in 1924) with a tremendously wide appeal. As examples of its commitment to cycling: it is affiliated to no fewer than fourteen cycling associations; it has twelve different secretaries (including one for 'Schoolpersons & Juniors' and one for 'Old Members'). This latter reveals the caring side of the club. Its handbook spells out some good sense to new members:

'*You can expect:*
Assistance and advice . . .
Free participation in . . .
Good prize values . . .
Standard medals for best performances . . .
Organised club runs . . .
Organised training runs . . .

The Club expects you to:
Cultivate the team spirit . . .
Not to give up if your performances are poor, but . . .
Attend club runs . . .
Assist with . . .
Be of good behaviour . . . ride cleanly . ... etc.'

Like all great clubs, it has its achievements to be proud of, its disappointments to come to terms with, its good times, its pathos. Young riders competing for the Tom Cannon trophy will know that he was a founder-member and first secretary. If they read the club's history (published in 1975), they will learn that he was born in 1898, went to war in his teens, suffered gassing which weakened his lungs and died after an illness following 'a paper-chase in . . . bitter November weather' aged thirty-one. A great young man. It is, too, a club of devotion (by 1975 one member had supplied and prepared free drinks and cakes for the committee for forty-one years) and great humour (in October each year you may ride 'The Twits 10'; or attempt a record ride of 21 miles 539 yards from Pratts Bottoms to Weald and back!).

London St Christopher's Catholic Cycling Club
Secretary: Malcolm Smith, 65 Pollard's Hill South, Norbury, London SW16 4LR

This lively club (founded in 1935) puts on a full programme of cycle touring, racing and social activities for its members. Clubroom facilities are available on Wedesday evenings (St Mary's Hall, Links Road, Mitcham, London SW17) and Fridays (St Wilfred's Hall, The Oratory, Brompton Road, South Kensington, London SW3) for films, talks, table tennis, refreshments, plenty of cycle-chat and other conversation, plus cinema and theatre trips, clubroom party, annual dinner, etc.

There are Sunday rides, one north and one south of the City, and club members know quick and quiet ways out to the countryside. Groups go away for weekend rides, either camping, hostelling or finding bed and breakfast accommodation, and opportunities exist for cycle tours abroad.

The Club caters for every type of racing cyclist, from novice to international class. It is specially keen on guiding those who want to take up racing and cooperates as fully as possible with parents of young members, giving advice on safety, insurance, equipment, etc. It is also very active in 'cyclists' rights' issues (see Chapter 2).

Membership is open to anyone who wants to join. As the Club itself says: 'We are a "Catholic" club in the sense that, for many members, the Christian faith is at the basis of activities like commitment to protection of life on the roads, commitment to a healthier and saner environment, to service to the cycling world generally. At the same time we have no sectarian bias; those who are not Catholics are every bit as warmly welcomed as those who are!'

Glade Cycling Club
Secretary: Mr K. McDonald, 20 Bentfield Gardens, Stansted, Essex

Glade Cycling Club (inaugurated in 1922) covers an area which includes north-east London and south-west Essex. It has clubroom facilities at Chingford and its Sunday club-runs start from Woodford.

Its active membership, ranging in age from thirteen to seventy, enjoys all forms of cycling. Its most illustrious period was in the mid 1970s when its cycle-racing prowess earned it the nickname: 'Gladys All Stars'. Its many competition records include some set by their schoolboy team and by tandems and tricycles. Perhaps their most notable success was achieved in the Tricycle Association National '25', when the Gladys All Stars were in first, second and third places, with the winner, Renny Stirling, setting an individual national record and the team establishing a national team record which still stands.

Tyne Road Club
General Secretary: Dennis Clayton, 7 Stoney Lane, Springwell Village, Gateshead NE9 7SJ

The Tyne Road Club (founded in 1938) operates mainly south of the river Tyne, providing facilities for cycle racing and club-runs. It was formed originally as an all-male hardriding club. During the War the entire membership, with the exception of one, was called up for service with the forces. The exception was sent on 'war-work' to another part of the country. The club had to go into abeyance but was re-formed in 1947.

It has a fine record of racing achievements, including:
1969–73, inclusive   RTTC National 24 hour Team Champions,

1970   2nd place RTTC National 24 hour Championship (individual),
2nd place VTTA National 24 hour Championship,
2nd place BCF National Schoolboys Pursuit Championship,

1972   2nd place RTTC National 24 hour Championship (individual),

1973   3rd place RTTC National 50 mile Championship (individual),

1974   1st place RTTC National Hill Climb Championship,

Northumberland & Durham CA Individual and Team Champions on numerous occasions.

Clifton Cycling Club
Secretary: Mr G. T. Parker, 20 The Garlands,
Rawcliffe Lane, York

This long-standing and still thriving club (formed in 1895) has a current membership of 170. Its long history is built on superlative service by its officials. It has produced many records and record breakers down the years, of which its proudest must be the selection of three of its members (Pete Smith, John Watson and Roy Cromack) to represent Great Britain at the Mexico Olympics in a team time trial. This is equivalent to an English league soccer club having eight or nine of its players in an England team. Roy went on to write his name indelibly in the record books by covering 507 miles in 24 hours on the undulating Mersey Roads course; a competition record still not beaten.

The club organises an enormous range of rides and races. These include a mixture of juvenile, junior, men's bicycle and tricycle, ladies, and veterans' time trials at 10, 15, 20, 25, 30, 50, and 100 miles, and 12 and 24 hours. There are also road races in juvenile, junior and senior categories, many standard rides (for example 230, 240 and 250 miles in 12 hours for EPNS, gilt and silver medals respectively) and The Yorkshire Alps Reliability Ride (see 'Reliability Rides' in Chapter 4).

Club members compete for nearly thirty different trophies.

But racing is only a part of this club, which describes its tours and club-runs as its backbone, and organises, also, a wide range of social functions.

A Selection of Smaller Enthusiast Clubs

300,000 Club
An exclusive club for those with documentary proof that they have cycled more than 300,000 miles, the idea of Frank E. Fischer, who in fifty-three years covered 457,000 miles. It now has thirty members (one woman) the greatest mileage being 799,405 by seventy-nine year old Tommy Chambers.

Cape Wrath Fellowship
This fellowship issues a certificate for those who cycle the 11 miles from the jetty 2 miles south of Durness village (Kyle of Durness) to the lighthouse at Cape Wrath, the furthest point north on mainland Britain. Contact: Rex Coley, via *Cycling* newspaper.

Pickwick Bicycle Club
This is the world's oldest bicycle club, founded in 1870. Many hundreds of members and guests attend the annual garden party held at London's Connaught Rooms each December.

Southern Veteran Cycle Club
This club was founded in 1955. In 1980, the SVCC's Silver Jubilee Century Ride, from St Giles,

Oxfordshire, to the Starley Memorial at Coventry, was filmed for television; twenty-seven riders set off at 4.30 a.m. on 52-inch ordinaries. The club holds several rallies each year in southern England and East Anglia. Membership Secretary: Douglas Marchent, 1 Popes Grove, Shirley, Croydon CR0 8AX.

Anerley Bicycle Club
This club had an unusual start. It was formed in 1881 as a hoop-bowling club for the boys at Dulwich College. Its centenary dinner and dance was held at Ewell, Surrey.

Over-the-Hill Gang
This informal group – prime mover Pete Matthews – are nearly all ex-first category racing cyclists and some are ex-Tour de France riders, including Stan Brittain. They meet on Sundays at Lydiate, Liverpool, ride for up to three hours and race for 10 miles, reliving the glory days of not so long ago. It is easy for them to joke about being 'over-the-hill' – they have had a good view from the top!

The Slowpoke Cycling Club
Open to adults over twenty-nine years of age, who are interested in any aspect of non-competitive cycling. In addition to organising very slow and short rides in quiet parts of the capital, it has a lively programme of social and cultural activities, and a (unique?) 24-hour Bicycle Road Rescue Service. The bimonthly newsletter is *Coasting*. Secretary: Ed Lord, 67 Liverpool Road, The Angel, Islington, London N1 0RW ☎ 01-837 7811.

Tandem Club
An enthusiast club which offers the usual facilities, plus a vital one for its specialist machine owners – a

postal spares service. The most popular national event is the Annual Rally (September) held in different parts of the country. Secretary: Pete Hallowell, 25 Hendred Way, Abingdon, Oxford OX14 2AN.

Pedal Club
Reorganised in 1952, it is the (still all-male) forum of British Cycling. Its monthly meeting, with an average attendance of sixty, is held at the Gascoigne Rooms, Waterloo, London SW1, and is addressed by invited speakers from the cycling world. Secretary: Alec Wingrave, 58 Tintern Road, Carshalton, Surrey.

Fellowship of Cycling Old Timers (FCOT)
This club was reconstituted in 1979 from the erstwhile Fellowship of Old-time Cyclists. Its secretary, Derek Roberts, also edits the bimonthly *Fellowship News*. Contact: Mr J. Shaw, 2 Westwood Road, Marlow, Buckinghamshire SL7 2AT ☎ Marlow 3235.

British Sponsored Cycling Clubs Association (BSCCA)
The BSCCA was created 'to encourage industry into the sport of cycling', and tries to obtain sponsorship for clubs. General Secretary: Mick Ives, 1 Coventry Road, Baginton, nr Coventry, Warwickshire.

24-hour Fellowship
This fellowship is open to anyone interested in long-distance riding and record breaking. Its members involve themselves as helpers during record-breaking attempts. Secretary: Les Lowe, 106 Jordan Avenue, Stretton, Burton-on-Trent ☎ Burton 42128.

Association of British Cycling Doctors (ABCD)
An association for doctors and 'para-medics'. Their annual meeting in October includes a 10-mile time

trial and 60-mile tour. Not a staid organisation at all, as can be inferred from the fact that the time trial in 1979 included an orthopaedic surgeon wearing a knickerbocker suit and a rose in his buttonhole. Contact: Rod Goodfellow, 267 Preston Road, Blackburn, Lancashire ☏ Blackburn 60260.

SWOMA and Potterers

Once upon a time . . . there was a 'National Cyclists' Union, South Western Section, London Centre Private Members and Sorian Road Club'. Got it! Well, the NCU SWS LCPM and SRC had Hardriders, Intermediate, Social and Potterers sections. Still with me? Then the NCU became BCF; exit all but: (a) The Potterers section, which still meets once a month. Secretary: Freddie Groves, 'Delfryn', 60 Brooke Forest, Fairlands, Guildford GU3 3JJ. (b) A new section called 'The South Western Older Members Association'. They recently celebrated their silver anniversary. Their annual dinner is held round a table at the annual dinner of Balham CC. Secretary: Grace Reynolds, 12 Tomlin Close, Staplehurst, Tonbridge, Kent TA12 0PH.

The Slob Cycling Club

And the eccentric? What about The Slob CC? Formed on 6 November 1982, it is 'a unique band of "no-hopers" who simply enjoy cycling but who would never disgrace the Club by winning races'. The first club event was Christmas 1982 at Salisbury Youth Hostel, supported by 100 per cent of the club's paid up members (five, I think). The object of the club is to promote the sport and pastime of cycling, catering particularly for slower and less serious riders, but with emphasis on social events. The pace the club sets, in every way, is very slow. In fact, if you write for membership you could be disqualified for showing that much initiative! Try contacting Terry Smith, 38 Manners Road, Southsea, Hampshire PO4 0BB.

40-plus Cycling Club
This club arranges some 300 easy paced rides (London and Home Counties) each year. Contact: Mrs G. D. Gardner, 16 Red House Lane, Bexleyheath, Kent DA6 8JD.

Many clubs have fascinating anecdotes connected with them. For example, the Nutwood CC was so called because its founder had always been fascinated by Rupert Bear.

2

CYCLISTS' RIGHTS

It is a basic right of all cyclists to use the roads safely and enjoyably. That right cannot always be assumed and must therefore be closely guarded.

There are many pressures in a rapidly changing world which would sweep away that right, either carelessly or deliberately. These pressures need to be studied, challenged, mitigated or annihilated, according to circumstances. In order to see clearly the need to maintain cyclists' rights, it will be necessary to look briefly at the following:

(a) The history of cycle use on the roads.
(b) The conflicts arising from road use and change.
(c) The forces which militate against cyclists' safety.

When cycling became popular during Victorian times it had few real problems to contend with. Speeds were limited, less by the design of the cycle or the fitness of the rider, than by the physical condition of the largely water-bound roads. There were, therefore, very few serious accidents caused to or by cyclists. Large numbers of riders were to be seen on the roads but traffic otherwise was light, the railways providing an alternative means of transport for travellers and trippers.

Cycles, therefore, became acceptable vehicles on all roads provided they were ridden carefully, conflict only arising with pedestrians and horsedrawn traffic, or the law, when riding became reckless.

After the turn of the twentieth century, the advent

of the motor vehicle brought rapid changes and ever-increasing danger for cyclists. Although cycling as a means of transport and enjoyment continued un-abated through a World War and a world-wide de-pression, enormous and damaging physical and social pressures were brought to bear on it.

Until the end of the First World War, the cycle had enjoyed a broad-based acceptability, both the work-ing and the emerging middle classes finding cycling an amusing diversion, if nothing more serious. As the horse gave way to the engine and relatively cheap motoring became available to the aspiring middle classes, the cycle was seen more and more as a work-ing class symbol, an attitude which persists more than half a century later. It was made to give way, literally, on the roads to a heavier, faster, breathless horse which threatened to sweep it aside if it did not move over.

For all the years that have passed since cycle and car first shared the road, little real progress has been made in understanding the merits of each, or in how to accommodate the needs of each. Rather, for too long, attitudes have been allowed to develop which see provision for motoring and the motorist as the only consideration when planning new roads, developing existing ones or repairing worn surfaces.

Beliefs have existed also, amongst municipal plan-ners, that cycles are out of date, that the views of cyclists can be ignored and that cyclists should be banned from the roads, less for their own safety than because they pose an obstacle to the fast flow of traffic. Where accidents to cyclists occur it is often less regretted than explained away that the cyclist himself was to blame for not having made himself visible enough, and what right did he have to be there in the first place since he paid no road tax?

Much more could be said, but it will be more useful

to describe particular problems faced by cyclists, looking at measures currently being taken to solve them. And I mean faced by *all* cyclists, because whether we race competitively, or tour leisurely, or ride with our children, or cycle to work, or go shopping on a bike, someone, somewhere, will try to stop us, or knock us down, or push us aside, or demean us. We all share the same roads and the same surfaces, meet the same hazards, obstacles and antagonistic attitudes because we are on two wheels. The forces, then, are against us all; the fight we wage is on behalf of us all. And we may take comfort in the fact that every day there are more of us; we are pressing our case more and more from a position of strength. Further, the whole world climate of ecology and conservation is swinging our way. The cycle is seen more and more as a sane, sensible means of transport in a world of dwindling energy resources.

It is in this positive frame of mind that the battle for cyclists' rights is being currently waged.

The Campaigners

Who, then, is campaigning for the rights of cyclists? What rights are they trying to protect or establish? And what are the problems being faced?

The campaigners come into several categories:
 (i) Pressure groups with a general interest in conservation, such as the Friends of the Earth.
 (ii) Action groups with a particular interest in cycling.
(iii) Cycling clubs and organisations.
(iv) Local authorities.

Friends of the Earth (FoE)

Friends of the Earth is an environmental pressure group funded by voluntary contributions. It has 250 groups and 17,000 supporters in the United Kingdom, and is part of a worldwide federation of national FoE groups. Bicycles and transport policy is just one of their several campaigns.

Many of the city and town cycling action groups referred to later are FoE groups, or benefit from cooperation with FoE. The organisation's contributions to cyclists' rights include the following:

(a) The creation of safe cycle routes in town and country alike. Some of the schemes under way or completed are described later.

(b) The support of local campaigns, thereby adding its experience and strength as a national organisation. This can have dramatic results. For example, the Watford FoE took issue with a district council whose plan for Rickmansworth scarcely mentioned cyclists. After pressure from the group, backed by all the expertise and 'clout' of FoE, the council made many concessions, including cycle entry down a one-way street, opening up bus lanes for cycle use, money for future cycle schemes and – not least – a very much improved official attitude to cyclists.

(c) The organisation of pot-hole campaigns, distributing massive numbers of printed cards. Any cyclist confronted by worn and dangerous surfaces completes a card and sends it to the local authority.

(d) It publicises cycling through various activities such as the popular Great British Bike Ride (qv).

FoE also publishes some useful material for cyclists:
1. *Way Ahead – The Bicycle Warrior's Handbook* (1978) Mike Hudson, 60pp. This explains the different techniques which can be used by individuals or

groups in persuading local authorities, etc., to make provision which encourages the use of bicycles.

2. *The Bicycle Planning Book* (1978) Mike Hudson, 154 pp. A wide-ranging book including chapters on bicycle usage, safety and law, bicycle planning abroad, current provision for cycling in the United Kingdom, and designing cycle facilities. There is a useful appendix detailing cycling facility provision in thirty-seven towns and cities, from Aberdeen to Swindon.

3. *The Bike is Back* (1980) Don Mathew, 24pp. A pamphlet stating a new cycling policy – aimed at Government – and a range of measures to implement it.

4. *On our Bikes* (1982) Caren Levy, 60pp. A survey of local authority cycle planning in Britain.

FoE also publishes a bimonthly *Bicycles Bulletin* devoted to issues of bicycles policy and planning matters.

See also: *'Bicycle Planning' – Policy and Practice*, Mike Hudson (The Architectural Press, 1982).

THEFACTS'. . . a fatal accident costs the local authority £120,000! '. . . a quarter of all road accidents are caused by poor road maintenance.'

THEREFORE: 'The FoE will take legal action against any lapse in statutory duty, because it considers that cuts in road maintenance are false economy and pose a dire threat to cyclists.'

Contact: Friends of the Earth, 377 City Road, London EC1V 1NA ☎ (01-837 0731).

City and Town Cycling Action Groups

Aberdeen Cyclists Action Group Assisted by Aberdeen University CC and Deeside Thistle RC, this group organised a cycle exhibition and a successful anti-pothole campaign.
Contact: Aberdeen Cyclists Action Group, c/o Chas Smith, 2a St Swithin's Street, Aberdeen.

Bedford's group is an association which includes the CTC, FoE and Bedfordshire RCC. The town boasts a national 'first': a set of cycle/pedestrian lights at a busy junction. The county council is active in several schemes, both completed and planned, in the town, including a three-quarters of a mile cycle/pedestrian way (Bromham Road), a 1-mile Fenlake cycle route and a recommended 25-mile cycle network.
Contact: Association of Bedford Cyclists, 11 Fetlock Close, Claphan, Bedford.

Belfast Cycling Action Group, c/o Ms Felicity Jones, 110 North Parade, Belfast ☎ Belfast 641476.

The *Birmingham Cycling Campaign* known as *Pushbikes*, has published a useful cycling guide (see Guides section in Chapter 11), holds monthly bike rides and plans a bike workshop.
Contact: Pushbikes, FoE Birmingham, 54–57 Allison Street, Digbeth, Birmingham ☎ 021-632 6909.

Bristol's group, called *Cyclebag*, was one of the earliest cycling action groups to make an impact. Formed in 1977, the group made itself known widely, the following year, when it organised a commuter race over a distance of 3 miles, between two girls on bikes, two in cars and two on a bus. In 1979 there was a similar race for shoppers, which the bikes won;

publicity being assured by Radio Bristol's along-the-route commentary. The bikes used were not racers either – the 'newest' was twenty-five years old, three-speed, with a handlebar basket, panniers and a cardboard box! Three days later a massive group of 600 riders invaded the city centre in support of their 'Pedals not Petrol' campaign.

By 1980 Cyclebag's membership was nearly 2,000, all able to receive 10 per cent discount at bike shops in the Avon area and benefit from a cyclists' insurance scheme. The previous year, volunteers had constructed a 5-mile cycleway, from Bitton to Bath, along the route of an old railway. This route has since been extended to Staplehill, with the hope that it will soon go all the way to Bristol.

In 1980 they began another project, a cycleway along the bank of the River Avon, from Ashton Gate to Pill. This route is along an old towpath and, unlike the railway line route above, had no foundation or drainage, and thus required much more effort. The cycleway begins at Prince St Bridge near the city centre, goes through the docks and past the national lifeboat museum and Brunel's ship, the SS *Great Britain*. It crosses the River Avon on the Ashton railway swing bridge, going under the Clifton suspension bridge and along the gorge. Despite the objections raised by councils, the scheme got under way with the moral and financial backing of the city council, and was complete by 1982.

Cyclebag continues its campaign to improve city centre facilities and a network of cycleways.
Contact: Cyclebag, 35 King Street, Bristol BS1 4DZ
☎ 0272 28893.

Cambridge have a dual organisation, aptly called *Biped*, whose aim is 'to maintain and extend the rights of all cyclists . . . to use their chosen mode of transport with a minimum of hindrance'. It aimed from the beginning to use the freedom released by the city's by-passes to implement cycleways; other intentions being to offer technical help through a bicycle workshop, legal advice and cycle insurance.

Within a couple of years it had won a 1½-mile cycle lane in Huntingdon Road, a 1-mile joint cycle/footway in Trumpington Road and a ¼-mile contraflow cycle lane in Downing Street in the city centre. Early figures show that nearly 2,000 cyclists use the latter each day, and a reduction in accidents in the area is indicated. When the Transport Minister visited the city, in October 1981, he highlighted the eleven schemes which had been implemented, four supported by Government. Cyclists everywhere will benefit if planners and highways engineers act on his message: 'Government is acutely aware of the need to promote cycle safety'. Contact: Biped, The Bath House, Gwydir Street, Cambridge ☎ 0223 312800.

Canterbury Cycling Group, 61 Cromwell Road, Canterbury, Kent CT1 3LE ☎ 0227 61784.

Cardiff Bicycle Planning Group, 36a Woodville Road, Cathays, Cardiff.

Chelmsford Cycling Action Group adopted a deliberate policy to foster positive relations with local organisations, including the County Highways Committee and the Chelmsford Society, part of whose interest includes the contribution of cycling to the easing of traffic problems. The group's main aim has been to establish a comprehensive network of cycleways in the hope also that cycling will be allowed in municipal parks. Progress has already been made: repair work has been completed on the cyclepath parallel to Bloomfield Road and joint cycle/pedestrian use established

of a subway under the Odeon Roundabout.
Contact: Chelmsford Cycling Action Group, Barny
Fleet, 17 Dane Road, Chelmsford, Essex.

Coventry FoE Cyclists Campaign, c/o Stewart Boyle,
Flat 1, 54 Warwick Place, Leamington Spa, Warwickshire ☎ Leamington 311108.

Edinburgh has a lively group called *Spokes.* In 1980 it
organised a 'go to work by bike' campaign, distributing 25,000 publicity leaflets. It makes a big impact at
rallies and festivals, organising its own and attending
others; its annual rally is held at Holyrood Park.

Its pressure forced the Lothian Regions Structure
Plan to include schemes for the safety of local cyclists.
In 1982 the Lothian Regional Council's first cyclists'/
pedestrians' way, along the defunct 'Innocent' rail
line, was opened by Lynda Chalker of the Depart-
ment of Transport.
Contact: The Lothian Cycle Campaign, 2A Ainslie
Place, Edinburgh EH3 6AR ☎ 031-225 6906.

Glasgow, in common with other Scottish organisations, struggles against the poverty of provision for
cyclists in that country (see a discussion on this later in
the chapter).
Contact: Glasgow Cyclists Campaign, 16 Newtown
Terrace, Glasgow.

Hull has a FoE group active on cyclists' behalf.
Contact: Hull FoE, c/o Stephen Noreiko, 6 Briarfield
Road, Hull HU5 4HX.

London Cycling Campaign includes, among its many
enterprises, a lobbying of the Greater London Council for safe cycle routes and cross-ways in the side
streets of the capital. It was a prime mover in the

provision of the 3-mile Ambassador Route from Paddington Station, through Hyde Park and over Chelsea
Bridge to Battersea. The route – so called, because it
passes many foreign embassies – crosses some of the
busiest roads in Britain and a feature is the provision
of cycle crossings at Albion and Albert Gates. Negotiations for the construction of the route were not only
long and tedious but interspersed throughout with
cries of 'impossible' from many influential quarters.
Its completion not only signals a victory for cyclists, it
shows what can be achieved if objections of all types
are patiently and relentlessly whittled away. Further,
if this is possible in London, nothing is impossible
elsewhere.

The Campaign uses various tactics to achieve its
aims. At a National Bike Rally it cited Camden as 'the
worst London Borough for pot-holes', and awarded it
a trophy – a battered wheel.

The group publishes its own magazine: *Daily
Cyclist*.
Contact: London Cycling Campaign, The Colombo
Street Centre, Colombo Street, London SE1 ☎ 01-
928 7220.

On *Merseyside* hard campaigning has brought a
multi-thousand-pound cycle route which links Liverpool University and its halls of residence with the city
centre. The campaign has the support of local MP
Anthony Steen. The Merseyside Friends of Cycling
publish their own hand-out *Pedal Press*, organise
publicity, such as sponsored rides, and have representation on the Merseyside Road Safety Committee.
(Local cyclists also contribute to, and take part in,
such activities as the Merseyside Cycling Festival.
Organised by the Voluntary Service Council and supported by cycling clubs and community organisations,
this massive eight-day entertainment includes fun

rides, family tours and dirt-track riding.)
Contact: Rolan Graham, Merseyside Friends of
Cycling, 20 Hilbre Road, Wirral LA8 3HH
☎ 051-625 9094.

Newcastle has a group called *Tynebikes* formed, at the
instigation of local authority planners, as an aid to
formal liaison with cyclists.
Contact: Shona Alexander, Newcastle Council for
Voluntary Service, MEA House, Ellison Place, New-
castle-upon-Tyne NE1 ☎ Newcastle 327445.

Norwich has a FoE group active on cyclists' behalf.
Unusual events tried by this group include a show,
based on music and drama, put on at different centres
in East Anglia. Between shows, the cyclists involved
rode modest distances, and camped out overnight.
Contact: Norwich FoE, Charing Cross Centre, St
John Maddermarket, Norwich ☎ Norwich 610993.

The *Nottingham* organisation is *Pedals*. Its early suc-
cesses included the filling in of pot-holes to reduce
hazards to cyclists, and the provision of cycle stands in
the city centre. The inertia of local authority in dealing with its call for cycle routes prompted it to prepare
a 48-page report (author: Hugh McClintock, a lec-
turer in town planning at Nottingham University)
aimed at the city, county and district councils. This
called for the establishing of over 100 miles of traffic-
free cycleways. The County's Environment Committee quickly approved plans for a cycle route from
Clifton to the city centre, the first of several that have
been promised.
Contact: Pedals, c/o Hugh McClintock, 162 Musters
Road, West Bridgford, Nottingham NG2 7AD ☎
0602 816206.

Rochdale Area Cycle Campaign originated from a trio of cyclists who were dismayed by frustrations and dangers caused by pot-holes. The group's aim is to make cycling safer in the town, especially by lobbying for improvements in road surfaces and traffic organisation, and in establishing cycle routes. It also hopes to improve the 32-mile towpath to the disused Rochdale canal for recreational use.
Contact: Rochdale Voluntary Action, 158 Drake Street, Rochdale ☏ Rochdale 31291.

Secretariat of Cycling Campaign Groups In 1980 seventeen cycling action groups banded themselves together in what was then called the Interim Secretariat of Cycling Campaign Groups. Coordinated from the London Cycling Campaign headquarters, it seeks to speak collectively, and thus in strength, to planning authorities.

Its first meeting, in March 1980 at the Bicycle Association Headquarters, considered mechanisms for organising a national campaign and discussed ways in which each group could learn from the others.

Sheffield Bike Campaign is a lively group. There is excellent cooperation both within the organisation (which involves FoE and CTC) and with the local authorities.

Two new cycle facilities have been introduced in the Havelock Housing Action Area, following consultations between Campaign officers, cycling groups and city engineers; and other plans are in hand.
Contact: Sheffield Bike Campaign, 110 Hemper Lane, Sheffield ☏ Sheffield 366847.

York has a FoE group. This city is, of course, renowned for its many cyclists. The campaign here dates back to 1975 and has worked to reduce the number of

vehicles in the narrow city-centre streets. The Fishergate Bar cycle crossing is a parallel signalled cycle/
pedestrian crossing of the inner ring road which allows
two-way cycle traffic only through Fishergate Bar.
Contact: York FoE, c/o Edgar Norton, 24 St Mary's,
York YO3 7DD ☏ 0904 52076.
☏

Cycling Clubs

The Cyclists' Touring Club

For over 100 years the CTC has been a significant
force in maintaining the rights of cyclists. Over the
years, it has both kept up the pressure to improve
provision for cyclists and resisted pressure which mili-
tates against them. Its history includes protracted
negotiations with railway authorities regarding the
transport of cycles on trains, talks which, down the
decades, have been at times acrimonious due to an
intransigent and antipathetic attitude at railway management level. In recent years some improvements
have been made, but propositions to British Rail have
yielded alternate hope and despair as they concede a
little, then withdraw.

Granted, the bicycle is not an easy parcel to convey.
To its owner it is a treasured possession, it must not be
handled carelessly and must be lodged within arm's or
eye's reach; to the porter/guard it is bulky and un-
wieldy, especially when loaded with panniers, demands a disproportionate amount of carriage space,
gets entangled with other cycles or parcels, and takes
time to load and unload. Hence the impasse.

Undaunted, despite 'HST-and-all-that', the CTC
battles on. (For the latest report on negotiations with
British Rail, see Alan Leng, 'Off the Rails', *Cycletouring* (August 1982).)

It has entered the fray on many types of issues, from
the 'lights on bikes' crisis to 'cycling on bridle roads'.

Its job has never been easy because, as mentioned elsewhere, it is trying to represent a membership which has conflicting views on almost every issue it contests.

It tackles the rights issue at several levels:

(a) As a member of cycling consortia, which both press for improvements and are consulted by Government for their views.

For example, early in 1980 the CCGB (of which the CTC is a member) circulated local authorities throughout Britain about the state of roads severely damaged by the previous bad winter. No fewer than sixty-five authorities replied, giving reasons for the bad surfaces and explaining their policy, giving details, too, of their repair plans and expenditure. Some had decided to transfer money from new road construction to road repair – an asset to cyclists.

The Department of Transport now asks the CTC and other cycling organisations to comment on draft proposals, for example their consultative paper issued in 1982, and proposed amendments to the Traffic Sign Regulations designed to help cyclists.

(b) It takes action on specific issues.

For example, the proposed by-pass at Hayes, Middlesex, was seen as a death-trap to cyclists. The CTC pressed for safer cycling provision, especially at the junction roundabouts. The GLC went much further, announcing the spending of £1 million on a new parallel 3½-mile cycle track with special subways at junctions.

Also, when a plan was made to ban cyclists from a new underpass in Millbank, under Vauxhall Bridge, the CTC objected strongly. The ban had been mooted for safety reasons due to heavy vehicles posing a danger to cyclists in the narrow tunnel. Instead, the lorries have been banned and cycling is allowed.

(c) Through its rights structure.

The CTC has traditionally monitored problems at local level through its District Associations and local information officers. These have, for example, kept an eye on statutory and legal notices in provincial and local newspapers. If a county council intends to downgrade a bridleway to a footpath, thereby preventing cycling along it, or to close a section of road due to new one-way regulations, or to bring in bye-laws restricting cycling on long-favoured cycling routes, etc., the DA would lodge objections and attend public meetings on behalf of local cyclists.

Recently, the CTC has appointed a national rights officer. It has also altered the brief of the local information officers, who now become local touring advisers – they know a great deal about their locality and can make its facilities known to cyclists coming to or through it. Instead, the DAs are appointing local rights officers to monitor issues and liaise with local authority planners.

London St Christopher's CCC

Here is an example of a lively cycling club entering into dialogue with local planning authorities. Not content for its members simply to ride or race their machines, it is aware that their freedom to do so is being constantly challenged, and their safety jeopardised.

Two examples of its campaign are:

(i) It responded to the Department of Transport's Consultative Paper on Cycling, based on members' direct experience of urban commuting by bicycle, recreational cycling and cycle racing. After commenting on the issues raised in the Paper, its members added a series of suggestions. The 4,500-word document included forty-nine responses to issues such as cycle schemes, improvements to trunk roads, training of child cyclists, the highway code and bicycle design.

Its own comments ranged from the 'lead in petrol' scandal to poor visibility of cyclists from lorry cabs.

(ii) Its latest report on current campaigns gives details of schemes in Barnet, Brent, Bromley, Croydon, Hailsham, Kingston and Lewisham, its representation on the GLC's Cycling Coordination Group, and its proposed South London Cyclists' Guide.

All rights issues, and the progress being made, are discussed once a month at the Mitcham clubroom (see Chapter 1).

Local Authorities

Although local authorities cannot be called 'campaigners' for cyclists' rights, it seems just to ally with the campaigners those local authorities whose provision for cyclists has been ready and totally sympathetic. It would be wrong, anyway, to imagine that 'the authorities' are generally antagonistic to the new urgency to provide for cyclists.

The fact is that provision for the motorcar – how to stop it choking the cities with its bulk and fumes, how to speed it through, where to park it – has drained the minds, energies and financial resources of many local authority planners for some decades.

With the growth in conservation awareness and the simultaneous disillusionment with the motorcar, due to its several anti-social disadvantages, local authorities have begun to realise that the bicycle is at least partly an answer to their problems.

Some authorities have been in the vanguard in planning for the cycle. Among these are the 'famous' examples: Stevenage New Town, where cycleways with flyovers and underpasses, which no motorcar has ever sullied, brought a new dimension to urban cycling and set standards for other places to emulate if they could; Peterborough, an expanding city which created inner-city cycleways on the Stevenage model, plus many miles of paint-marked cycle tracks along its broad new ring roads.

It is true that these and other pioneering authorities are notable because rare, but fortunately they set precedents which other towns and cities find hard to gainsay in the face of determined pressure from cycling organisations. Yet it must be stressed, the best schemes for cyclists have come not from those authorities which have been blatantly or unremittingly badgered by aggressive pressure; rather it has been where reason, good sense, good humour and cooperative professionalism have prevailed that cycling has been given the attention it deserves.

After all, money and labour are required for most of the changes needed, and both of these are almost exclusively controlled by local and national Goverment. It is no easy task in times of dwindling cash to persuade the authorities to divert money into new and maybe untried schemes. The most successful cycling campaigners in their dealings with authority know that where sympathy exists, it must be fostered by a responsible, carefully reasoned approach; where antipathy prevails, it must be shown to be ridiculous by arguments rationally and politely presented. So sensitive can the job of the cycling campaigner be in negotiating with Government, that he needs the support of all cyclists.

Where the aims of campaigner and urban planner coincide, things begin to happen, as in Stevenage and Peterborough. If only there were planners of *that* calibre and depth of vision throughout Britain. Just a handful of other examples can be fitted in.

In 1980 Sheffield opened a new cycle track – the Darnall Cycle Route – which links housing areas with the Darnall shopping centre, a school and an industrial estate in the Lower Don Valley. The route takes cyclists off busier roads and follows the line of two roads now closed. There are hopes to extend it soon. The city has several other plans, including: a cycle route in the Sharrow–Abbeydale–Heeley area, cycle/pedestrian routes through subways and across busy roads, and contra-flow lanes in one-way streets. For details of current and planned facilities contact: The Department of Planning and Design, Sheffield City Council, Town Hall, Sheffield.

In Derby an experimental scheme is being tried which has parallels in many towns and cities – the cyclists may use the contra-flow bus lanes in the city centre. The city council advised bus drivers and the general public that cyclists would be using the lanes. In addition, it has published an illustrated leaflet in which it explains the scheme and the thinking behind it, frankly admitting that the present fast roads make city cycling 'neither easy nor convenient'.

Oxford City Council has acted to cut down accidents involving cycles, a prominent city councillor publicly declaring his shame that the council had taken so long to improve conditions for cyclists. It is intended to introduce a programme to provide an extensive network of cycle lanes.

Cycling in the capital has never been easy and has become increasingly dangerous even for the fearless and experienced rider; many would-be cyclists have been driven from the road by the sheer speed and volume of the traffic. All so-called improvements have made the roads wider or faster so as to gobble up more and more vehicles.

Pressure by the CTC, the LCC and others in recent years has led to radical changes in the cycling policy of the Greater London Council, even if the many schemes they are considering take a long time to implement. Money set aside for cycling schemes – nil prior to 1980 – was only £25,000 in that year, but had exploded to a reasonable £1.7m (1 per cent of the transport budget) per year by 1982. The GLC has also set up a separate unit of officers to consider cycle schemes. The team has increased from an initial four to fourteen, currently considering well over 100 cycle schemes in central London and the Boroughs. To help rationalise the provision and put cyclists into the planning system, a consultative group has been set up. This includes GLC members and national and capital cycling groups. (For a helpful article on GLC policy see Nick Lester, 'Transports of Delight in the Capital', *Bicycle Magazine*, (November 1982).)

The Other View

Not all cyclists are happy about current trends in cyclists' rights. Reservations arise mostly in two areas:

(i) Some cyclists object in principle to non-specialist cyclists (pressure groups) acting on behalf of cyclists, reckoning it to be arrogant – 'leave cycling to cyclists'. They also fear that the heavyweight tactics will sour the relationships which have been built up steadily between 'true' cycling organisations and the authorities. They do not accept the complaint that nothing seems to be happening, nor that aggressive action will bring quicker or better results.

(ii) A strongly held view, in fact part of the policy of the CTC itself, is that cyclists must always be allowed to cycle on the public highway. They fear that if too many special routes are provided, cyclists will not only be forced to use them instead of using the adjacent roads, but will become less and less welcome on roads generally.

Already cyclists are banned from motorways – where they would not want to be anyway – and they are increasingly being excluded from city and town-centre high streets in pedestrian areas where buses, delivery vehicles, etc., are allowed to drive. Cyclists do, of course, have access to bridle roads, canal towpaths, etc., where motor traffic is not allowed, and this in part counterbalances the exclusive provision of some roads for vehicles.

For an interesting pair of articles giving opposing views see: Roy Stockdill, 'Beware the Pressure Groups' and Brian Stout, 'Ride a Bike – Safe from Traffic', *Cycling* (11 July 1981).

Background reading
- (a) J. Abbiss and L. Lumsden, *Route Causes* (Macdonald & Evans), a 44pp guide to participation in public transport plans
- (b) A. Barker, *Public Participation in Britain* (Macdonald & Evans)
- (c) See also FoE publications mentioned earlier

For a safety organisation's response to the Ministry of Transport's Consultative Paper, contact RoSPA, who make the important point in their conclusion: 'More cycling need not mean more cycling accidents'.

3

CYCLE RACES

Cycle racing has a history almost as long as cycling itself. But it has never been so exciting, so popular or so complex a sport as at the present day.

Not only are more and more people taking to the cycle for sport and recreation but the range of competitive opportunity is growing steadily. The purpose of this chapter is to describe the types of cycle races which have established themselves on the sporting calendar, including the most recent innovations.

Simply put, the different ways that racing can occur are:

(a) alone against the clock,
(b) in groups competitively, on roads or closed circuits.

That is where the simplicity ends. The great fascination of cycle racing is the bewildering variety of races built on that basic framework.

The organisation of races can also be put simply: all time trials are run according to the regulations of the RTTC; all road and track events are under the control of the BCF (and SCU). But this hides the wealth of variety, both of affiliated clubs which organise races under these controlling bodies and of the races themselves.

The following types of racing are described in some detail:

Time trials
Road races
Cyclo-cross

Track racing
Motocross
Cycle speedway

Time Trials

These are races against the clock, described in the RTTC handbook as: 'organised competitive events in which the riders start in separate units (individual or group) at different times of the day, and the placings are determined entirely by elapsed time or distance covered'.

Individual riders start at minute intervals, with longer intervals in team time trials, up to three minutes for four-man teams. As any number of 'units' up to 120 may take part, it could be 2 hours before the last rider goes off. This means that in a 10-mile race the first rider may finish in just over 20 minutes but have to wait 2 hours to compare his time with that of all other riders.

Later riders have the advantage of knowing many of the times they have to beat in order to win, and can be encouraged through their ride by enthusiastic spectators: 'Ray, you've got 9 seconds over Tony', etc. They may also have another advantage. Most time trials start early in the morning. At 7 a.m. in March it could be gloomy, cold, icy, foggy, etc., but by 9 a.m. it could be glorious sunshine with a dry road surface. On the other hand, the weather could worsen during the race.

A real problem is wind – its speed and variation. Most time trials are out and back. For example, a 25-mile race could be 12½ miles down a dual carriageway, turning at a roundabout, and 12½ miles back, the start and finish often being on a less busy side road where marshals' cars, the tea wagon, etc., can be safely parked.

This out and back system evens out the terrain and wind. A so-called straight out course will be in one direction only. The rides on this will be faster because advantage can be taken of the gradient and prevailing wind.

A team time trial will be referred to as two-up, four-up, etc., according to the number of riders in the team. The time for the race in the latter will be taken as that of the third rider in the group, so that it is vital that the team keeps together.

One beauty of the time trial, accounting for its popularity, is that although the race has a winner, a rider who has no hope of winning can try to better his own time. Another attraction for competitors concerns the character side of the race. In France, where cycle racing is the national sport, the time trial is known as the 'Race of Truth' because a rider is not motivated by other riders in close proximity. A different kind of strength of character is thus required and the rider finds out the 'truth' of his strengths and weaknesses.

In time trials, as in all races, a handicap system can be worked, and this gives a chance for the also-rans to gain honours.

Riders may compete for places in each race, for personal bests, for club awards and for national RTTC trophies. The usual time trial distances are 10, 25, 50, and 100 miles, and times of 12 and 24 hours.

When one considers that races can be organised for individuals and teams, amateurs and professionals, men and women, juniors, juveniles and veterans; over all the above distances and more; on roads and closed circuits, rough stuff and hill climbs; using bicycles, tricycles, tandems, etc., at club or national level, it is clear that every taste can be catered for.

Some clubs now put on 'family' time trials in which juniors, women, veterans and seniors all take part, a continuous afternoon's racing involving anything up to 250 riders. It is not unusual for a son or daughter, mother and father, and grandparents to take part in a single afternoon event.

(See also RTTC, Chapter 1.)

Road Races

These, organised under BCF rules, are: 'competitive events in which direct racing between the riders is permitted and in which placings are determined by the physical order of finishing'.

Most races are on the open road, on circuits which are covered several times. For example, an 8-mile circuit ridden twelve-plus times for a 100-mile race. Tactics are very important in such races and each rider will use his particular strengths, skills and experience to advantage.

Where races start in town centres or within built-up areas of high traffic density the racing 'proper' will not begin until outside the de-restriction signs, or by prior agreement with the local police.

In contrast to time trialling, much higher speeds can be attained by groups of racing cyclists, each rider contributing perhaps 20–30 pedal revolutions at very high speed while at the front before slipping away to the left and back, the next rider then coming through for his turn. This method allows each rider to work at maximum output for a brief period before taking 'rest' from the buffeting wind as the group rotates anti-clockwise until his turn comes round again. A break-away team could use this tactic to forge well ahead of straggling individuals.

It is very important in road racing to conserve energy by this pacing method of sheltering behind other riders. The man who wins a road race is often the one who has cannily saved his strength in this way, yet ideally not to the point of shirking his share of the work.

Both stamina and sprinting ability are needed. It is the sprinting away that is the excitement of road racing. It can be encouraged by the organisers offering prizes – called primes – for the first rider past a certain point, or to the rider who completes a circuit fastest, etc.

A sprint can split a field. One minute, forty riders can be riding along complacently, as if on a weekend tour, the next, there is a rider sprinting furiously, a dozen riders, not taken entirely by surprise, pedalling with equal fury to get back on his wheel, and the rest struggling, angry, maybe soon to be demoralised and beaten. If the sprinter goes off the front early in the race he could soon be hauled in by the chasing group (peloton) so he must be sure to choose his moment carefully. If he is confident of having the sprint, and the stamina, to maintain the advantage it gives him, he will be looking for the opportunity to accelerate.

A good place is at a sharp bend. Then he can be spurting away when the others behind cannot see him to retaliate until he has opened a disheartening gap. Another place is on a hill. Many racing cyclists fear hills, so a strong rider who likes them can totally shatter the majority of his rivals by surging forward at the moment the others ease off the pedals to gear down.

Road race tactics are complex and defy explanation in the short space available here.

A particularly interesting type of road race is the 'Criterium', sometimes called a 'Kermesse'. This is held on a closed road circuit, most spectacularly in a city centre at festival time. It usually lasts 1 hour and 1 lap. A 20-mile race can have the riders zipping round the streets up to forty times. One can imagine the reaction of the riders when the race commentator announces over the public address system: 'The Mayor has offered a £20 prime to the first rider past the Town Hall'.

(See also BCF, Chapter 1.)

Cyclo-Cross

Clubs affiliated to the BCCA organise cyclo-cross races under the rules of the Association, which is itself affiliated to the BCF. Cyclo-cross is a competitive cross-country race on bicycles. Events are usually scratch races where riders start together and cover a preselected course. This will vary from flat grass fields to muddy tracks and steep slopes, and will often go through woods, streams and other natural and contrived obstacles, so that great skill is needed in cycle control and in knowing where to ride or carry the bike.

Star- and clover-leaf-shaped courses, which allow the maximum use of minimum area, provide circuits requiring up to ten laps for a 5-mile race.

The starting line, as in mass-start marathon running, is as wide as possible to enable the riders to line up abreast, with an open space of some 200 yards before they need to funnel on to the narrow part of the course. Then it is go, go, go, through whatever ingenious conditions nature and the course organiser have devised, the first rider over the line being the winner and all riders finishing in that same lap.

Cyclo-cross is a gruelling race and the lighter the bike the better. Many young riders take part, so the emphasis is not on the expensive but on the simple. In any case, the more complicated the cycle, the heavier it will be, the more trouble, the more dangerous. So the machine is stripped of lamps, brackets, saddlebags, mudguards, pump, bell, etc. A single freewheel or fixed cog is sometimes preferable to variable gears but if gears are used handlebar changers enable them to be selected without letting go of the 'bars.

The chain must be tenser than normal to avoid 'unshipping' when bouncing along. Mud on the pedals causes slipping, and toeclips (double to prevent them folding on impact) are useful. Tyres with a good tread and slightly under-inflated (as for icy roads) should be used. All of these and many more tips are soon learned by the 'cross rider. No expensive clothing is required but it should be warm, close fitting and comfortable. A special precaution is necessary with shoes because these can come off if the going is sticky. It is usual to have a loop sewn at the back for a strap to be passed through and tied over the instep.

(See also BCCA, Chapter 1.)

Track Racing

Track racing takes place under BCF regulations. The tracks are usually short (333 metres), steeply-banked wooden structures as at Leicester, the scene of international track championships.

Track racing is now among the most popular aspects of the sport and the 1982 World Cycling Championships brought spectacular TV coverage of track racing to homes throughout Europe. Track events are non-stop action, with races switching from bicycle to tandem, from individuals to teams, from races so short that you could almost miss them if you blink to 'sixes' – six-day-long competitions. The various races at championship level include:

Sprint

This is a marvellous cat-and-mouse race of three laps between two riders (but there may be three or four in earlier heats). The excitement is in the surprise tactics used by riders to outwit their opponents. These tactics include riding in the front man's slipstream so close behind as to bemuse him – he is not sure where the attack will come from, or when. Another is to slow the race down. At international level it is not unusual to see top bikers, such as world champion Sergei Kopylov of Russia, balancing stock still for minutes on end. Sometimes during the final lap one rider will break, timing his swoop down the banking to leave his opponent behind – if he can. The times of the riders over the last 200 metres are recorded. Repechage (or repeat) heats enable beaten riders in fast heats to qualify for later heats.

Pursuit

In this event the riders start at opposite sides of the track and pursue each other like greyhound and hare in a gruelling race of usually twelve laps (4,000 metres), depending on the circuit length. The riders use fixed gears to give a pedalling rate of approximately 100 revolutions per minute, rhythm and sustained high speed being crucial. Then it is a case of hammering away trying to knock seconds off the opponent. In rare cases of miss-matching a pursuiter will catch his man (race over) but usually there are just seconds between the riders as they cross their respective finishing lines. In team pursuiting there is the added spectacle as the leading rider, having taken the sting of the wind for half a lap, swings up the banking and down again to take a breather at the back of the team, the second man then doing his stint. In this event it is the time of the third man (of the four) which is counted at the line.

Time Trials

These are usually over 1,000 metres, the ride being completed in about 60 seconds. Riders go alone. They must decide: is it a steady pounding ride with a final all-out burst, or all-out burst from the start, which risks the legs going to jelly near the end?

Points

In these races, over various distances, points are given to the leading rider at fixed positions, say at each half-lap or lap, with double points for the final sprint.

Devils

This is a shortened form of 'devil-take-the-hindmost'. A large bunch of riders sets off on a multi-lap race. At each lap the last man over the line has to drop out. When every rider but three has been eliminated these sprint for the final lap. It is a very popular race among spectators.

Madisons

Madison racing takes its name from Madison Square Gardens in New York, where riders raced to literal exhaustion for six days. These 'sixes' as they are now known continue, but have been drastically altered, the main feature being the Madison relay ride between pairs of competitors.

The most spectacular six-day racing event has been the Skol-6, held on a short, steeply-banked wooden track specially built to fit the Empire Pool, Wembley.

Here the relay riders zip round the track at terrific speed, each relieving rider being slung literally into the race by the rider who has just completed his stint. The latter takes a breather, riding slowly round the track, before he himself is flung into action for yet another lung-bursting couple of laps.

Mini-Madisons have been introduced at some tracks. These are short sharp events of anything between fifteen and twenty-one laps, with sprints every third lap. They give an opportunity for more riders, and especially young and inexperienced riders, to get on to the track. Less experienced riders benefit from being paired with more experienced riders.

Motor Paced

In these events, each rider keeps behind a motor cycle, popularly a Derny machine. The pace provided by these machines and the shielding effect results in races of considerable speed and excitement. The 'Keirin' is currently very popular. It is a scratch race lasting four laps behind a single Derny which gradually increases its speed. When the last lap arrives it is going full throttle. It then swings off the track and the bunch sprints for the winning post.

The 'Omnium', as its name implies, is an all-round test of cycling skill – the tetrathlon of track riding. Riders compete with each other over four chosen events, such as short distance sprinting, long distance points and Derny racing, and time trials. Points accumulate to decide the winner.

(See also BCF, Chapter 1.)

Motocross, or BMX

This is hailed by the organisers, UK-BMX, as the fastest growing and most significant youth sport in the country. It consists of riders, aged five years to over twenty, racing light, strong, 20-inch-wheel cycles down a short closed circuit of 400 metres. The course can include a number of jumps, turns and other obstacles to add to competitor and spectator interest. Usually six to eight riders take part in heats of one circuit, called a moto. The competitors are given points according to their position in three motos, the riders with the lowest points then going into quarter-finals and semifinals and then the final.

Great emphasis is put on safety. Riders must wear full protective clothing including lightweight leathèrs, helmet, goggles and long-sleeved jerseys strengthened at the elbows.

The organisers of motocross stress the ecological benefits of the sport – it is on solid ground, causes no pollution, and damage to the track is minimal. And it is sheer fun. Because riders start so young and the demands upon riding skill are rigorous, competitors learn to handle the bikes safely. They learn also the responsibilities of using and maintaining their bikes and the importance of fair play and sportsmanship.

(See also UK-BMX, Chapter 1.)

NB The advent of BMX in Britain was accompanied by much discussion as to its merits and durability. As examples, see articles:

(a) 'Robert Garbutt, 'BMX – Big Boom or Damp Squib', *Cycling* (19 July 1980)
(b) Richard Grant, 'A Tiger by the Tail', *Cycling* (16 May 1981)
(c) BMX Review, *Bicycle Magazine* (January 1982)

Cyclo-Trials

This is the latest variation on the BMX theme, the official organising body being UK-BMX. It is like cyclo-cross but control, not speed, is the object. (Most young cyclists have 'played' it unofficially: riding a bike over the roughest ground possible without putting a foot down.)

A course will be divided into observed sections, each section having hazards such as steep banks, rocks, logs, bends and cambers. Each rider is watched through a section. If he touches the ground (dabs) with his feet he loses a mark, losing two marks for two or more dabs, and three marks if he stops, falls off or leaves the course. The rider usually does three laps, having three attempts at each section.

The first cyclo-trial in the United Kingdom was at Heaton Park, Manchester, when an 800-metre course of eleven sections through rolling woodland attracted a field of forty-two young riders.

All cycle sport produces skilled riders. Cyclo-trials should provide a spin-off asset to cycling if it produces very young riders who can cycle slowly without wobbling on busy roads.

Cycle Speedway

This independent cycle sport, only slightly similar to speedway, is not dirt-track riding. Races or 'heats' take place in an anti-clockwise direction from a standing start on an oval, usually shale-surfaced track. Four riders race four laps and the first past the chequered flag wins. The tracks are about 100 metres long and sometimes have shallow banking. In addition to the black-and-white chequered flag, a yellow flag is used to signal one lap to go. The riders are started from an upwards-rising gate. They must be adequately protected from injury by being fully clothed from the neck down, including gloves, and a crash helmet for tarmac surfaces.

As in all cycle racing, high standards of safety are required. The machine must be simple, with no adornments or projections. The small 18–21 inch frame has 26 × 1⅜ inch wheels with gripster tyres. Gears are not permitted, nor fixed wheels, nor multiple chainrings – just a low-geared single freewheel for rapid acceleration from the start and out of the bends. The bikes usually have straight forks which shortens the wheelbase and helps cornering. For the same reason the cranks are short at about 6¾ inches.

Team racing is the life-blood of the sport and major leagues operate in all regions of the United Kingdom. Matches take place at weekends. In addition to regular fixtures, invitation events such as four-team tournaments, best pairs and individual competitions add variety to the racing calendar. The British Championships are held each year, the top sixty-four riders competing for the title British Cycle Speedway Champion. There are also categories: Schoolboy (Under-15), Junior (Under-18) and Youth (Under-21).

(See also Cycle Speedway Council, Chapter 1.)

Cycling National Championships

1. *RTTC (Time Trials)*
10 miles	(Women), (Schoolboys)
25 miles	(Women), (Men), (Juniors)
50 miles	(Women), (Men)
100 miles	(Women), (Men)
12 hours	(Men)
Team (4)	(Men)
24 hours	(Men)
Hill Climb	(Men)

2. *Cyclo-Cross*
   Amateur (Men)
   Professional (Men)
   Veterans
3. *BCF (Road Races)*
   Amateur (Men), (Women), (Juniors)
   Professional Road Race
   Professional Criterium
4. *BCF (Track)*

Professional	1,000 metre Sprint
	5,000 metre Pursuit
	Omnium
	1 hour Motor-paced
Amateur	Club Team Pursuit 4,000 metre
	1,000 metre Sprint
	4,000 metre Pursuit
	20 kilometre Points
	50 kilometre Points
	1 kilometre Time Trial
	80 kilometre Madison
	50 kilometre Motor-paced
	Tandem Sprint
Women	500 metre Sprint
	3,000 metre Pursuit
	15 kilometre Points
Junior	500 metre Sprint
	3,000 metre Pursuit
	30 kilometre Points
	1 kilometre Time Trial
Schoolboy	500 metre Sprint
	500 metre Time Trial
	2,000 metre Pursuit

4

CYCLE RIDES

A significant feature of the bicycle revival has been the growth of organised rides. So-called 'standard' rides have been popular for many years. There are many variations on the 'standard' theme but the main types are:

(a) Reliability Rides
(b) Randonnées
(c) Place-to-Place, or Circuits

The last have developed along less rigorous lines, as will be explained later.

It must be emphasised that none of these are races. Although distances and times may be specified, rules are deliberately included to prevent the ride from developing into a race. Most rides of these types are designed to test a rider's ability to pace himself over a distance, and are based solidly upon enjoyment.

Variations on the reliability ride are the standard ride itself, and the tourist trial. These three may be loosely defined as follows:

(i) *The standard ride* is a no-frills affair in which a rider must cover a specified distance within a specified time. For example, 100 miles in 8 hours. It makes no difference if the rider paces himself finely, covering the distance in 7 hours 59 minutes, or if he shoots off at 'evens' (20 mph) intent on doing a personal best of under 5 hours; he still qualifies for a standard ride award. There are various distances and times to suit a cross section of riding abilities and aspirations.

Thus a club may put on a standard ride on a 50-mile

circuit, with riders being required to cover one circuit in 3, 4 or 5 hours, others committing themselves to two circuits (100 miles) in say 6, 7 or 8 hours. The course may be marshalled, with club members at tricky junctions to guide the riders along, or a route sheet may be issued and the route itself way-marked.

(ii) *The reliability ride* is a standard ride but with tighter controls on pace. It will have similar distances and times, but, as will be seen from the rules given later, there is an emphasis on proper pace. To ensure this even resting times for refreshments en route may be specified, and the route will be closely monitored by marshals so that sprinting, racing, or idling does not occur. The reliability ride is currently very popular and will be discussed more fully later.

(iii) *The tourist trial* is a reliability ride to which the organiser can add almost anything! Thus, competitors may be required to take part in pace-judging sections, freewheeling sections, map reading, quizzes on general knowledge, local/regional geographical or historical knowledge, technical cycling knowledge, etc. In addition, marshals – some hidden – may award points for cycling style, correct use of gears, and so on.

The tourist trials have an added impetus each year as CTC District Associations organise qualifying heats in their areas for the national tourist trial contest, called the BCTC (British Cycle Tourist Competition), an event held annually in different parts of the British Isles.

The Reliability Ride

Distances and times now vary considerably owing to the appeal of the rides to families and very young riders as well as to the more experienced riders.

Whereas at one time the 100-in-8 was regarded as a

minimum 'qualification' for any self-respecting tourist, now there are distances of as low as 10 miles to be covered in 3 hours.

This latter distance may seem hopelessly easy, but for someone very young, or someone taking up or returning to cycling, and perhaps even having a kiddi-seat on the machine, and having to scale hills, it is no mean achievement on the way to increased stamina and longer rides. An advantage of the reliability ride is that it allows group riding and the occasion becomes a social event. It also engenders confidence in the inexperienced who rely on the support and direction of more able riders.

Apart from such obvious basic rules as having cycles in sound mechanical condition, fitted with two brakes, reflector, etc., further regulations have been formulated by the Cycling Council of Great Britain. These must be followed by any organiser or club staging such rides, but participants should also be fully aware of them.

All the regulations can be found in the handbooks of the RTTC, BCF, SCU, etc., but a few are mentioned here for interest:

1. Reliability rides are not races, and shall be organised simply to require that each entrant must ride over a specified distance within an agreed time.

2. In the case of entrants riding in groups, no one group should at any time consist of more than twenty riders.

3. The organiser must appoint travelling controllers to ensure that these regulations are being obeyed.

4. Where riders are started in groups, the interval between each group should not be less than five minutes.

5. The route of a reliability ride shall be so planned

that it will necessitate all-round ability and not sheer speed.

6. No reliability ride shall be promoted which requires the participants to maintain an average speed of more than 18 mph. 'Average riding speed' means the average speed when actually riding; all periods allowed for meals, etc., must be deducted from the total time.

7. The only 'result' that shall be issued shall be a list of riders who have completed the route within the specified time. No finishing times or order of finishing may be published.

Randonnées (or Brevet Rides)

These originated in Italy in 1897 and became most popular in France. A 'brevet' is a ticket, which is both the entry requirement and the award for completing the ride. On the Continent, entry to the most prestigious 'randonneurs' (for example, the Paris–Brest–Paris) has to be earned by completing specified shorter rides, but the brevet rides in Britain (organised by AUK) have developed along less formal lines.

As with the reliability rides, there is a wide variety of randonnées. Thus the End to End is a 1,400-kilometre (869-mile) ride from Land's End to John o'Groats; the Aberystwyth to Great Yarmouth, 500 kilometres (310½ miles); and the Poole–Yarmouth–Abersytwyth–Poole triangle is 1,000 kilometres (621 miles) with several starting points. Riding at 100 kilometres (62 miles) each day the End to End takes a fortnight.

Grimpeur events are hill climbs (for example 200-kilometre (124-mile) events over Exmoor involving

10,000 feet of climbing) with *Super-Grimpeur* for those who like the climbing to hurt.

At the family and young rider level, there are various distances: 600 kilometres (373 miles) down to 200 kilometres (124 miles), the Popular Brevet of 100 kilometres (62 miles), and the Petit Brevet of 50 kilometres (31 miles).

Medallions are often awarded as an extra token of success.

For a fuller account of randonnée events, their history and development, by John Nicholas, see *Bicycle Times* 26 and 27 (July and August 1982); or contact AUK (qv).

For advice on riding the events by two experienced randonneurs, see *Cycletouring* (June 1982). In this article the following seven points, made by Paul de Viver, founder of the magazine *Le Cycliste*, are quoted:

1. Light meals and frequent. Eat before getting hungry, drink before getting thirsty.
2. Never ride until so tired that you can't eat or sleep.
3. Few stops and short, so as not to lose your cycling rhythm.
4. Put on extra clothing before getting cold; take some off before getting hot.
5. No smoking or alcohol during the ride.
6. Never rush. Ride within yourself, especially at first when you feel strong and may be tempted to force the pace.
7. Never pedal to show off.

Place-to-Place

These are to cycling what the London Marathon and similar events are to jogging. They are fair distance – some very long distance – mass 'family' rides, for sheer pleasure. Unlike the above two types of organised rides, they are less structured and time limits are often not set.

They have, inevitably, been used to full effect by the cycling rights and environmental lobbies as a means of showing the public at large, and local and national Government, that cycling cannot be dismissed as a minority sport.

Most such rides begin in town or city centres. Everything that is needed to get the riders safely and enjoyably to the end is provided, apart from the cycles. The rides go to other towns or cities, usually by a rural route to avoid traffic, or loop back to the place where the rides started.

Space allows a short description of only a few of these so-called 'standard' rides. Anyone interested in taking part is advised to scan the cycling press because rides are being organised throughout Britain, and few people will be more than a few minutes' cycling from an event of one sort or another. The more ambitious, who will only be content to ride in the most popular or longest events, will find that special trains or other travel facilities are provided by the organisers – at a reasonable charge – to get riders to or from the event.

Some Reliability Rides

Those interested in reliability rides would be well advised to join a section of their local CTC District Association because the DA will almost certainly organise several trials during the year, most particularly in spring and autumn when the days are cooler. However, all types of cycling clubs and organisations put on reliability rides and the following illustrate the range of options available.

The New Forest Cycling Club organised a reliability trial 'with a difference'. Starting at 10.30 a.m. from the Rising Sun, near New Milton, the ride of 45 miles through the Forest, on both metalled roads and forest tracks, included a pub lunch stop 'to admire the scenery'. Some families and groups used the stop to have a picnic meal. The entry fee was nominal and certificates were awarded for finishers in $3\frac{1}{2}$, $4\frac{1}{2}$ and $5\frac{1}{2}$ hours. A very leisurely pace.

This sort of trial gives an opportunity to cycle in places one might otherwise not tackle. With routes clearly defined, plenty of marshals on hand to keep the riders on the right track, fellow cyclists to meet and chat to en route, and marvellous scenery, plus the achievement of finishing and maybe a souvenir award at the end, it holds all the ingredients for a superb day. All for a few pence.

The Lancaster Cycle Club, and Friends of the Earth, organised a 62-mile reliability trial starting at 9.30, 10.30 and 11.30 a.m., and 30- and 40-mile family rides, starting at 10 and 11 a.m., all rides finishing at 3 p.m. The rides were in the grounds of Hornsea Pottery, Lancaster (0524 68444), which extend over 40 acres of landscaped parkland with a variety of family entertainment available, making this occasion a great family day out. In addition, it is typical of many similar such rides on closed circuits – it gives freedom of mind from the problems of motor traffic.

Bann Wheelers organised the first reliability trial in Northern Ireland for many years, in February 1981, with almost all Northern Ireland's clubs represented. The distances were 70 or 100 miles for seniors, with 30 miles for women and juniors. Starting from Collin School, the route lay along the Murder Hole Road to Limavady with a 30-mile leg to Londonderry for the full-distance riders, then to Dungivan, via the Glenshane Pass to Maghera, Portglenone, Kilrea, and back to Collin.

The notion of club riders taking part over a distance of 100 miles may seem daunting to unattached and less-confident riders, but the 70-mile route is not so far under the steady pace conditions of a reliability trial which, after all, is designed to set a standard with enough sweat to justify eventual feelings of real achievement.

Some people may hanker after really gruelling reliability rides. They are to be found. Consider the Clifton Cycling Club's 'Yorkshire Alps Reliability Ride'. This ride, as a variation from the club's organised runs and races, has been recognised since 1960, but only about a dozen riders have qualified for certificates in that time. Participants are timed away by a club official at Exhibition Square, York. They then proceed via Scotch Corner, Bowes Moor, Tan Hill, Thwaite, Buttertubs, Hawes, Fleet Moss, Grassington, Pateley Bridge and Knaresborough; thence back to Exhibition Square.

There are two standards for this 160-mile course – 12 hours and 14 hours. The best time to date is by Messrs Bramham, Treweek and Hails, in April 1960, of 11 hours 10 minutes. There is only one snag to this ride – if you complete it successfully in the time a fee of 5p is payable on claim.

A great many less formal organised events are being put on now. Those who feel they do not qualify for full-blooded reliability trials, or find them unsuitable for their circumstances, should not have far to go for something less demanding.

The Ulster Bike Day, organised by the Northern

Ireland Cycling Federation, provides a good spread of rides. This annual event raises money for the Ulster Cancer Foundation. It has a main tour on a circular 100-mile route, starting from Belfast at 7 a.m. and finishing 7, 8, 9 or 10 hours later. The Lough Neath Monster Tour has starting points at Belfast, Craigavon, Cookstown and Antrim on its 100-mile circuit. In addition, clubs affiliated to the NICF organise local rides of up to 20 miles at an easy pace.

Some Randonnées

There are now so many randonnées being organised that the growth in popularity of these rides can only be described as an explosion. As mentioned earlier, the first such randonnée was organised as a qualifying ride for the Paris–Brest–Paris; it was the Windsor–Chester–Windsor. So successful has been the growth of British randonnées, that British participation in Continental events often surpasses national entry. British randonnées are now an end in themselves.

The freedom of randonnées in part accounts for their success; they are founded on 'Allé Libre' principles, 'free riding' or 'go as you please'.

The 'Heart of Kent Bike Ride', in October 1981, was just such an event. This 50-kilometre (31-mile) ride, designed for beginners and families, started and finished at East Malling Institute Hall, and riders could go off alone or in groups any time between 9 and 11 a.m. The route took in the rural villages of Brenchley and Goudhurst and the hop fields around Marden. Those with plenty of energy were free to do an extra 50-kilometre ride to Tenterden and back.

A more strenuous test was that organised by the Bristol CTC and the Clevedon & District RC and called the 'Herefordshire Brevet'. It was a 200-

kilometre (124-mile) ride from Bristol to Leominster and back.

An interesting variation to look out for is the all-through-the-night randonnée, an example being the 'Wessex CTC's 300-kilometre (186-mile) Breakfast Brevet' organised by John Burrows. The event started at 2 a.m. (yes!) from Christchurch in Hampshire, moving north-east along moonlit and traffic-free roads (one benefit of the night ride) through Cranborne and Tollard Royal, with the wide open Salisbury Plain to the north, to Shaftesbury. By now it was 4.30 a.m., well into dawn, and time for refreshment at a control point. Then it was due north for another 72.5 kilometres (45 miles) to reach Malmesbury in north Wiltshire by 8 a.m., and breakfast, before swinging south for the final legs home.

It is essential on such a ride that each randonneur has studied the route carefully beforehand. Rides up to 500 kilometres (310 miles) are very long rides and are bound to put the cyclist in countryside that he is unfamiliar with. If he gets separated from a group, or the bike has serious mechanical trouble, he could be lost or stranded a long way from home with no-one awake to give him directions.

An event which is bound to grow in popularity is the 'CTC's National Randonnée'. The 1982 '400-kilometre Brevet des Randonneurs' was open to all cyclists, not just CTC members. The distance, equivalent to about 250 miles, could be covered in any time between 14 and 27 hours, with 24 hours being the average time. Starting during the afternoon from Charterhouse School near the CTC's national headquarters, at Godalming in Surrey, the route took minor roads westwards to Overton and then along the Test Valley to a control point at a refreshment stop, then another shortly afterwards, at Salisbury Youth Hostel. In addition to these fixed control points, where the brevet cards were signed and stamped, there were secret controls and roving controllers to validate claims.

The route then went south over Cranborne Chase to Wimborne and Upton, and then to Swanage where refreshments could be taken in a buffet car, courtesy of the Railway Preservation Society. Some riders took the opportunity of a swim in the sea. By this stage, it was dark and lights were on, but the route north-east through Bournemouth and the New Forest was on main roads which were easy to follow and fairly quiet. The remaining miles through Fareham and Chichester were covered during the night, most riders finishing at or shortly after dawn.

The Harrogate Show and Festival now includes AUDAX events in its programme. Typical randonnées are two 200-kilometre (124-mile) rides which went west and east of the city in 1981. The first ride went up Nidderdale to Pateley Bridge, then through some tough up-hill sections via Hebden, Grassington and Conistone to Wharfedale, and yet more tough miles before Wensleydale was reached. The route went north towards Richmond before swinging back down to Leyburn and the river Ure and the final miles to the finish.

The second ride took to the rolling hills of the Yorkshire wolds, between Harrogate and Malton, sticking to the superb lanes and through tiny villages en route to Bridlington. The riders were treated to refreshments on Flamborough Head before beginning the second leg back home through Driffield and York.

Some Place-to-Place Rides

The event which captures the attention of the media most, and involves the greatest number of riders, is the now annual 'London to Brighton' ride.

Starting from Hyde Park at 7.30 a.m., one morning in early May, the riders go via Mitcham, Nutfield, Turner's Hill (this is the lunch stop, at 34 miles) and Lindfield to Ditchling Beacon above Brighton (58 miles) before descending to the seaside town in triumph. The event was started in 1976 by John Potter, a cycle dealer from Bath, and money is raised by sponsorship for the British Heart Foundation.

Intending participants can get full details of forthcoming rides from either: John's Bikes, 1 Cleveland Place East, London Road, Bath, Avon ☎ Bath 310859; or The London Cycling Campaign, 48 William IV Street, London W1.

A place-to-place ride in Scotland, which should not be missed by local cyclists, is the annual 'Edinburgh to St Andrews' ride organised by Spokes, the Lothians Cycling Campaign, in early September. The nearly 60-mile ride starts at 9 a.m. from the Mound, Edinburgh, and goes via the Forth Bridge cycle path and Kinross to its seaside destination. Facilities provided by the organisers include refreshment stops en route, luggage carrying, accommodation at St Andrews, return transport and entertainment. The accent is on an enjoyable, leisurely ride.

The 'Great Midlands Bike Ride' is of similar length (about 60 miles). Organised by Pushbikes (Birmingham Cycling Campaign), with beginners in mind, it now attracts many hundreds of participants. The route runs in a figure of eight from Birmingham's Rag Market to Stratford-on-Avon and back. It starts at 9 a.m., has a refreshment stop in the middle, and includes entertainment and fun of various kinds.

Much of this easy-paced June ride, suitable for beginners, families and experienced tourists alike, is through superb rural lanes in Shakespeare country.
Contact: ☎ 021-643 4141 – daytime.

There are many similar rides up and down the country.

'The Great Dorset Bike Ride' was first held in June 1979, and enjoyed its third repeat in 1982. Starting from Dorchester at 9 a.m., lunch is usually taken at Poole harbour, followed by a ferry crossing to Studland and a visit to Corfe Castle, then returning to Dorchester. An evening 'bicycle bop' has been held in support of Greenpeace, the conservation organisation.
Contact: Bike Ride, c/o Cornucopia Wholefoods, High West Street, Dorchester, Dorset.

'The Great Nottingham Bike Ride', in June 1982, started from the site of the Goose Fair, north of the city, and went via Calverton to Newark, passing through the superb Sherwood Forest area and rolling countryside around Southwell; a distance of nearly 30 miles.
Contact: 33 Tavistock Drive, Mapperley Park, Nottingham.

A September ride is the 'Beacon Bike Ride', in its third year in 1982, named after its promoter – Beacon Radio, and organised by Penn CC and Wolverhampton Lions. The 30-mile oval ride, avoiding main roads, starts and finishes at Wolverhampton Stadium, Aldersley, and visits Compton, Trysull, Claverley, Bridgnorth, Worfield and Pattingham. There is a lunch stop in Severn Park, Bridgnorth, with refreshments along the way, provided by MacDonald's fast food restaurants' 'Orange Bowl' service, at Claverley and Pattingham. Riders are encouraged to raise money by sponsorship for MIND, the National Association for Mental Health.

Contact: 1 Whitehall Road, Penn, Wolverhampton ☎ 0902 339489.

'Bike Events' provide rides on the same theme with variations; single day and week-end rides, train-assisted to beauty spots.

For example, they chartered a train from London, aptly labelled 'The Bicycle Belle' and took 300 passengers and their bikes to Eridge in Sussex for a choice of nine (10–60 miles) rides in the Sussex and Kent lanes.

The train left London Bridge station at 8.45 a.m., passengers then being entertained by actors from Art-on-the-Run, part of the National Theatre, Bath. At Eridge the party split up according to choice: a 30-mile ride to Rudyard Kipling's home and back, a 40-mile stint to Ashdown Forest and the Bluebell Railway, or a fast zip to the sea at Rye, 30 miles away.

An example of their weekend events is the 'Shrewsbury Ride'. A special train runs from London, reaching Shrewsbury by midday Saturday. Rides in the countryside around the famous flower city end at Berrington Hall, about 5 miles from the city centre, where the riders camp. Entertainment is provided at a Saturday evening barbecue, with more rides of varying lengths on the Sunday.

Contact: Bike Events, 66 Walcot Street, Bath, Avon.

One of the greatest place-to-place rides, of course, is the 'Land's End to John o'Groats' (End to End) ride. Ever since a wheel-chasing-a-wheel was invented, adventurous cyclists have been pedalling the length of Britain. It has been done by lone cyclists, groups of cyclists, handicapped cyclists; record attempts have been made by the fastest on two wheels, on three wheels, on tandem, on penny-farthing; by the youngest, the oldest, etc.

Each year the ride gets slightly shorter as roads are straightened, bridges thrown across estuaries, and so on. But as often as it is mastered it remains a magnet to aspirants and an achievement to accomplishers.

Because it has been ridden so often and so variously, it seems almost impertinent to single out particular rides, but to do so will act as a tribute to the many who have done it and as a spur to those on the brink of trying.

Perhaps the ride which has captured the imagination most in recent years is 'The Great British Bike Ride'. This will be contrasted and compared with another – a ride of real courage. Both rides did the route 'top-to-bottom' (a Jogle) in August and September 1981 respectively, and both were sponsored. The GBBR was for Friends of the Earth, whilst Mollie and Tom Pugh were raising money for Cancer Research.

The GBBR was limited to two hundred cyclists, as many women as men, ranging in age from eleven years to seventy-three, beginners and experienced riders, including doctors, mechanics, carpenters, nurses, physiotherapists, a hydro-geologist – the whole gamut. They travelled by train to the north and were accompanied on the ride south by a car carrying spares, a van with shelters and tent for meals, two vans of food and a lorry loaded with gear. One can just imagine the cavalcade, the colour, the swish and zip, the excitement. Cafe owners were astonished as the first fifty riders bought up the whole stock of chocolate, with a hundred and fifty still queuing, and were equally astonished as the famished riders asked for seven eggs and chips! Whole bus queues clapped, especially when they saw the blind participants on a triplet, or Graham Gates, who pedalled doggedly day after day on his high ordinary (penny-farthing).

The ride took about three weeks, at a 50-miles-a-day average. Main roads were used only when unavoidable, otherwise the route deliberately took to scenic rural roads. Organised by Bike Events it included theatricals by Art-on-the-Run, providing entertainment for riders and the public, and to help 'sell' the event through the press. Though limited to the two hundred, other cyclists were welcome to ride some or all of the way, so long as they made their own arrangements for feeding and sleeping. (This was continued into 1982, the organisers inviting prospective 'tag-alongs' to phone for details of the various camp sites en route, and to join the ride for any distance they desired. This seems a good way of preparing for the real thing in subsequent years.)

Contact: Bike Events, 66 Walcot Street, Bath, Avon ☎ 0225 65786.

Background reading: See, for example, *Bicycle Magazine* (November/December 1981) – two articles.

Tom and Mollie Pugh travelled by sleeper train to Inverness, and then to Wick, leaving a 17-mile cycle ride to the start proper. Their ride through Scotland involved more than they would have wished of rain, headwinds and walking. For meals they invariably picnicked in a sheltered spot, and found bed-and-breakfast accommodation as they went along. Only at Warrington did they have difficulty, and the local police found them digs in Lovely Lane. They kept on in leisurely style, finding time to divert to beauty spots or historical monuments, and having two rest days en route. By cruel misfortune they had to contend with gale force winds and rainstorms in the west country right to the end, having covered a distance of 1,082 miles. Intending long-distance riders who have little experience should bear such unpredictables as the weather very carefully in mind when making plans. Tom and Mollie, who were seventy-seven and seventy-two years old respectively at the time of the ride, raised several hundreds of pounds for Cancer Research.

Background reading: 'Not Too Old for the End to End', *Cycling World* (January 1982).

Those planning an assault on the End to End will find the following publication useful: *Three for Two was No Picnic*, an accurate description of their ride by Chris Raine and Barry Parslow, 2 Wendroc Close, Truro, Cornwall. (Please send an appropriate donation to cover costs and postage, all proceeds going to research into muscular dystrophy.) For interest, compare the routes taken by the GBBR, Tom and Mollie Pugh, and Eric Tremaine, who set a record tricycle ride.

GBBR	THE PUGHS	ERIC TREMAINE
John o'Groats	John o'Groats	Land's End
Helmsdale	Berriedale	Exeter
Tain	Bonar Bridge	Bristol
Inverness	Maryburgh	Gloucester
Dalwhinnie	Carrbridge	Worcester
Edinburgh	Dalwhinnie	Wolverhampton
Barnard Castle	Crieff	Warrington
Lancaster	Dunfermline	Preston
Liverpool	Peebles	Lancaster
Shrewsbury	Lockerbie	Kendal
Brecon	Keswick	Penrith
Chepstow	Warrington	Carlisle
Bath	Buckley	Gretna
Taunton	Chirbury	Beattock
Exeter	Leominster	Edinburgh
Tavistock	Redbrook	Perth
Truro	Weston-super-Mare	Inverness
Land's End	Tiverton	Bonar Bridge
	Lewdon	John o'Groats
(About 3 weeks)	Mitchell	
	Land's End	(2 days
		6 hours
	(About 3 weeks)	18 minutes)

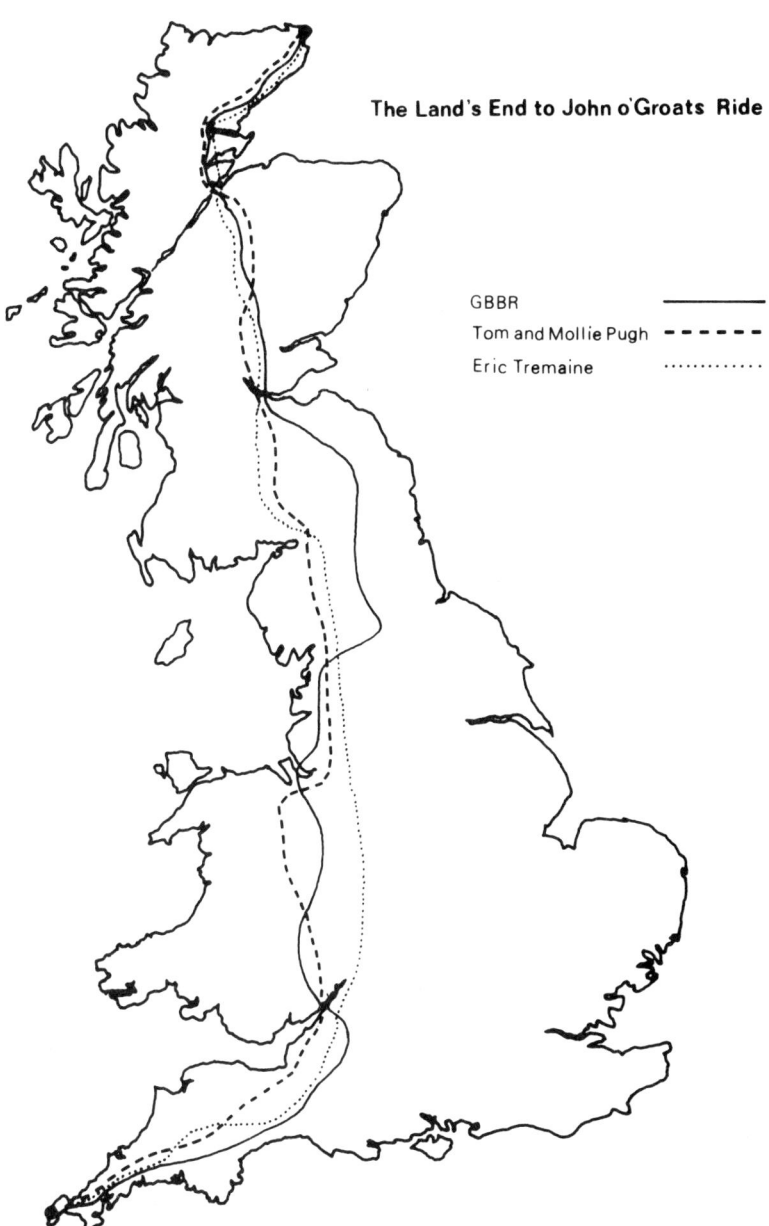

The Land's End to John o'Groats Ride

GBBR —————
Tom and Mollie Pugh ———————
Eric Tremaine ················

Other Organised Rides

There are, of course, many other sorts of organised rides, sufficient to satisfy the demands of all 'grades' of cyclists. Those who want to take part in regular rides with a group should join one of the many clubs described elsewhere in this book, especially the various sections of the CTC District Associations. Most sections have experience of organising rides which goes back through several generations. They know where best to ride, how to prepare for all possibilities, who to put in charge of the ride, etc. They usually issue pre-ride duplicated route sheets, which are a boon if cyclists become separated from the group due to puncture or other mechanical trouble.

They know how to cater for different cycling temperaments and can cope both with the 'fast boys', who might split a group by riding far ahead, and with the stragglers, who might become disheartened at being left behind or at slowing the party down. Either they will organise separate rides for different groups or build loops into the ride so that different groups can choose how far to go.

For example, the Loughborough section of the Leicestershire DA organises both 30- and 130-mile standard rides, and their members attend the York Rally and the CTC's Birthday Rides, and even the international AIT rallies all over the world; yet most of the section's day-rides are round trips of about 30 miles enjoyed by families and younger riders.

As an example of the loop principle, the Leicestershire DA's annual President's Ride starts and finishes at the same place, but has three different objectives en route. A recent ride began at Syston, on the Fosse Way north of Leicester, all the riders setting off together eastwards. Group A shortly swung northeast to visit Burrough Hill, an iron-age encampment and favourite picnic area, the rest carrying on to Oakham, county town of the former county of Rutland. Group B stayed here, while Group C went on to complete a circuit of the massive Rutland Water. By the time the groups came together again later, they had cycled 21, 38 or 46 miles respectively.

Look out, too, for special events, particularly annual weekends put on by CTC District Associations. Two examples are:

(a) 'Golden Beeches', put on by the South Buckinghamshire DA, is a weekend in late autumn, very informal and very popular, of rides in the Chiltern hills led by local knowledgeable cyclists. Based on Great Kingshill, near High Wycombe, it includes an evening slide show.

(b) 'The Lincoln Cyclists Weekend' is in September, and draws cyclists from a very wide area. The cyclists stay at Lincoln youth hostel, local bed-and-breakfast accommodation or camp. There are guided rides and a longer tour, many family attractions in the afternoons, and an evening slide show.

5

CYCLEWAYS

In addition to the open road, the cyclist has a wide variety of routes open to him: gated roads and green lanes, tracks across heath and hills, bridle roads, canal paths, old railway lines, routes through forest and parkland, and so on. The freedom of the open road though, must not be undervalued. The more the cyclist uses commuter and other roads the more he will have his needs recognised by authorities. And, once he can cope with the traffic, he will find plenty of satisfaction just being awheel, frustrations and annoyances from fumes and noise, and all!

The purpose of this chapter, however, is to give information about the scope of facilities available, mostly longer rides varying from road-based routes to genuine rough stuff.

The Open Road

The keen cyclist will always be curious to ride round the next corner, just to see what is there. This insatiable inquisitiveness will inevitably lead him further afield – and the cycle tourist is born. A good deal of literature is becoming available to help the cyclist plan a tour. Route guides for the whole of Britain, and its parts, may be purchased in bookshops or through the cycling press, and more details are given in Chapter 11.

Local authorities are cooperating with other statutory and voluntary bodies in introducing cycling schemes in their locality. Three examples are given to illustrate the breadth of provision.

The North Lancashire Cycleway

This 130-mile cycleway is a massive circuit of the Forest of Bowland, taking in the superb Ribble and Lune Valleys, and linking, in the north, with the even longer Cumbria Cycleway. The route was selected by the Lancashire County Council, with advice from local FoE and CTC groups, and keeps to lightly-used minor roads as much as possible.

It may be joined at any point, cycled in one un-broken ride, occupy a week of leisurely riding, or even sampled in small pieces.

Suppose it is joined at Longridge (on the B6243) in the shadow of Beacon Fell – conveniently reached from Blackburn, Accrington, Burnley, Preston, etc., – and followed clockwise. This is the Ribble Valley, its river running west towards the sea, dominated on the north by the Forest of Bowland.

The Cycleway goes west as far as Wrea Green, 3 miles from Blackpool, then turns north, crosses the exposed Fylde plain and goes via Cockerham and Crook o'Lune into the beautiful Vale of Lune near Lancaster. It keeps on north through Carnforth to Arnside where it fuses with the Cumbria Cycleway as far as Kirkby Lonsdale. Here it turns south and again enters the Vale of Lune; then begins a long, hard but rewarding section over the Bowland Fells, with the Pennines to the west, including the massive peaks of Whernside, Ingleborough and Pen-y-Ghent (see Three Peaks Race), and down again via Slaidburn into Ribblesdale.

Scenery and facilities for short and long stay visitors are excellent. Apart from the magnificent rural, forest and moorland scenery, there are nearby towns, villages and coastal resorts, country parks, picnic areas, nature trails and an abundance of historic sites.

Those wishing to travel to the area by car or public transport may hire cycles from:

Arnside South Cumbria Cycle Hire, Souton, Silverdale Road ☎ Arnside 761929

Morecambe Surrey Cycles, 9 Morecambe Street ☎ Morecambe 422559

Ribble Valley For the Clitheroe, Longridge and Whalley areas, cycles and equipment may be hired from the Adult Education Service ☎ Whalley 2717

Two convenient youth hostels are: Arnside (superior grade) Slaidburn (simple)

For free details of the Cycleway, contact: County Planning Department, East Cliff County Offices, Preston, Lancashire PR1 3EX.

They also publish the leaflets:

  (a) *Lancashire Farm and Country Holidays (Ribble Valley)* (17 farmhouse and cottage accommodation addresses),
  (b) *Lancashire Farm and Country Holidays (Vale of Lune)* (12 farmhouse and caravan addresses).

The Cumbria Cycleway

This, the first long distance cycleway in Britain, was opened in 1980.

It is a 250-mile circular route around the Lake District on (mainly) quiet roads, bridleways and footpaths.

It follows the coast going north from Barrow-in-Furness, via Whitehaven and Workington to the Solway Firth, and Carlisle. After Brampton it turns south, passing near Penrith, skirting the Yorkshire Dales National Park, and back to Barrow.

(It can, of course, be combined with the Lancashire Cycleway to form a very long figure of eight route.)
Background reading: Robin Muir, 'Cumbrian Reflection', *Cycling World* (November 1981)

The route is clearly way-marked and would form an ideal week's cycling, with plenty of places to stay (farmhouses, bed-and-breakfast guest houses and youth hostels). The local Tourist Board supplies a list of addresses of cycle hire firms, and a map and guide to the cycleway.
Contact: Cumbria Tourist Board, Ellerthwaite, Windermere, Cumbria.

Cycling Around Rutland

The Leicestershire County Council have published a series of three leaflets *Cycling Around Rutland*, describing routes radiating from the beautiful Rutland Water. The routes, which keep deliberately away from busy roads, vary in length from 10 to 25 miles. Some of the most popular routes are those which keep within the confines of the massive reservoir on tracks made available to cyclists by the Anglian Water Authority.
Contact the Council at: Department of Planning and Transportation, Glenfield, Leicester. (See also Cycle Hire, Chapter 9.)

Recreational Paths

The Countryside Commission encourages local authorities to provide and maintain paths for recreational use. Some of the paths are open to cyclists (regrettably few, as yet) and these are listed below. Most of them are way-marked. Application to the appropriate county council for details will be answered by a variety of publications, from simple maps to detailed guidebooks.

Cheshire

Wirral Way (about 12 miles) West Kirby to Hooton through Wirral Country Park.
Contact: Head Ranger, Wirral Country Park, Station Road, Thurstaton, Wirral L67 0HN.

Derbyshire

High Peak Trail (about 17 miles) Follows the old Cromford and High Peak Railway through superb countryside from Cromford to Dowlow, connecting with the Tissington Trail.
Tissington Trail (about 13 miles) Uses the former Buxton–Ashbourne railway line from Ashbourne to Parsley Hay, where it connects with the High Peak Trail.
Contact: Derbyshire County Council Planning Department, Matlock, Derbyshire DE4 3AG (free leaflet, send stamped addressed envelope, for Tissington Trail) or Peak District National Park, Aldern House, Baslow Road, Bakewell, Derbyshire DE4 1AE (leaflets are available for High Peak and Tissington Trails).

NB A useful triangular ride of about 40 miles can be made using these two trails and the B5305 Ashbourne to Wirksworth road.
(See Chapter 9 for some idea of the considerable provision of cycle hire in the Peak District.)

Durham

Bishop Brandon Walk (about 10 miles) From Bishop Auckland across the River Wear on the Newton Cap

Viaduct, through farmland and along the Wear Valley to Broompark Picnic Site.

Deerness Valley Walk (about 7 miles) From Broompark Picnic Site along the Deerness Valley towards Crook.

Derwent Walk (about 10½ miles) Swalwell on Tyneside to Blackhill, near Consett. Part of a large country park with riverside picnic area, woodlands and views of the Derwent Valley.

Contact: Durham County Council Planning Department, County Hall, Durham DH1 5UF (three free leaflets; send large stamped addressed envelope).

East Sussex

Forest Way (about 9½ miles) From Groombridge to East Grinstead along the route of a disused railway line.

Contact: East Sussex County Council, County Estates Department, 42 St Anne's Crescent, Lewes, East Sussex (price of leaflet on application).

These few 'cycling-allowed' paths, from a Countryside Commission list of sixty-five for walkers seem extremely thin. However, things are improving almost daily. Also, cyclists can use their initiative with paths in their locality, following such paths with the help of bridleways and roads en route. Two examples are:

(i) *The Viking Way* (140 miles) From Humber Bridge South Humberside to Oakham, Leicestershire. This is a route incorporating very ancient trackways. It is way-marked throughout with a Viking helmet. The Way was established by the Lincolnshire County Council in cooperation with the Humberside County Council and Leicestershire County Council. Coming south from Humber Bridge, it traverses the

Lincolnshire Wolds Area of Outstanding Natural Beauty, via Caistor, Horncastle and Woodhall Spa, west to Lincoln and then south again past Grantham. Although designed for ramblers, the Way can be followed easily by cyclists along the numerous adjacent country lanes, where the Way uses metalled roads including the Roman Ermine Street, bridleways, such green lanes as the famous Sewstern Lane in north Leicestershire, and disused railways, for example the 7½-mile Spa Trail from Horncastle to Woodhall Spa.

See the article: 'Humber Byways' by Barry Barton, *Cycletouring* (December 1981), on the 40-mile High Street route from Humber Bridge to Horncastle.

Contacts: Director of Technical Services, Humberside County Council, Eastgate, Beverley, North Humberside (free leaflet);

County Land Agent, Lincolnshire County Council, County Hall, Lincoln (six leaflets are available, being phased out and replaced by a single booklet);

County Planning Officer, Leicestershire County Council, County Hall, Glenfield, Leicester (leaflet available).

(ii) *The Peddars Way* (15½ miles) This is a similar ancient trackway, in north Norfolk; however, it has a significant difference – it is arrow straight. Waymarked along its entire length, it includes roads, lanes and arable fields. It begins in the north at Ringstead, 2 miles south of Hunstanton, and goes via Littleport, Fring, Harpley and the Massinghams to the castle and priory town of Castle Acre. It is rideable most of the way, any short tough stretches being compensated for by superb scenery.

See article in *Cycling* (August 1, 1981) – Alan Mepham.

Long-Distance Routes

Cyclists can make use of Britain's long-distance routes. Twelve such routes have been proposed by the Countryside Commission and approved by the Secretary of State for the Environment. Eleven of them are now open, and leaflets are available from the Commission.

Contact: Countryside Commission, John Dower House, Crescent Place, Cheltenham, Gloucestershire GL50 3RA.

Some parts of all the routes are open to cyclists and one – the South Downs Way – is a bridleway and thus available to bike-riders along its entire length of 81 miles.

The South Downs Way extends from Eastbourne, right across Sussex to Petersfield in Hampshire. No fewer than six youth hostels stand on or near the route, enabling a very leisurely pace to maximise the enjoyment of the superb scenery and historical features. The South Downs is an Area of Outstanding Natural Beauty and the profusion of wildlife, combined with such fascinating features as the prehistoric fort at Devil's Dyke, and a rough stuff mastery of Beacon Hill, will make the slowest progress the most enjoyable.

Prepare in the armchair with maps, and the book *South Downs Way*, by Sean Jennett (HMSO).

A similar long distance path – though not all bridleway – is *The Ridgeway Path*. This 84-mile route spans the North Wessex Downs and the Chilterns, from west of Marlborough, in Wiltshire, to east of Tring, in Hertfordshire. Some parts, as along the Icknield Way, are metalled road, but other parts are stony and rough and progress will be slow. The Path starts in the west near the prehistoric stone circle of Avebury, following a very old route nearly due east, passing the

famous Uffington White Horse and many other fascinating relics, from ancient castle sites to more recent
windmills. Also along the route are National Trust
houses, country parks and national nature reserves, as
well as adjacent towns and cities. The Ridgeway Path
is only a few minutes' pedalling from Swindon, Reading, High Wycombe, Aylesbury, etc., and thus becomes easily accessible for a train-assisted day's ride
along particular sections.

The other nine routes are:

1. *The Pennine Way* Read John Aizlewood's
   account of West London DA's (Camden section) Easter Tour. They took the bridleway
   from Langden Beck to Dufton. It gives a
   graphic account of snow drifts and peat bogs,
   and brings home the rigours and realities of
   Pennine conditions and the need to go well
   equipped. (See *Cycletouring* (December
   1980).)
2. *The Cleveland Way*
3. *The Pembrokeshire Coast Path*
4. *Offa's Dyke Path* NB John Holland covered
   the 176 miles in 61 hours, including hurdling
   800 stiles between Chepstow and Prestatyn,
   carrying his bike through blackthorn bushes
   and gorse in his shorts, getting lost four times,
   getting three punctures, a wasp sting and a
   shock from an electric fence. John has also
   tackled the *West Midlands Way* (170 miles)
   and the 94-mile *West Highlands Way* from
   Milngavie to Fort William. On the latter he
   cooperated with the bike, riding it for 64 miles
   and carrying it for 30 miles.
5. *North Downs Way* See the article 'Pilgrim's
   Way', by Peter Knottley, *Cycling*, (10 January
   1981).

6–9. *South-West Peninsula Coast Path* comprising: (6) Somerset and North Devon, (7) Cornwall, (8) South Devon, (9) Dorset.
See the article 'Riding the Dorset Downs', by Maurice Teal, *Cycling* (6 December 1980).

Rough Stuff

This is the loose term applied to riding on unmetalled surfaces. The surface can include that of good solid bridleways, stony farm tracks, field roads, green lanes, moorland and mountain tracks, and the rugged land where an undaunted wheel can follow the hoof-marks of sheep or a stream's bed.

Apart from the centres of cities, therefore (I will come to canals later), there is rough stuff available everywhere, and this short section serves simply to whet the appetite so that readers can go out and discover their own rough stuff, and make it a much used, much loved retreat from the constraints of everyday life.

You will need, of course, a philosophical attitude to the occasional puncture, to mud on the rims, to a bit of walking, to fairly heavy duty equipment, but . . .

The Yorkshire Dales

There is a route (O.S. map 98), much used by cyclists, along Swaledale near the Durham border. It contains those happy ingredients: a combination of rough stuff and country lanes; and alternative roads to add variety and give choice to suit conditions.

The route can be a 'circular' one taking both northern and southern ways along the River Swale. Starting at Thwaite, 10 miles south-east of Kirkby Stephen on

the B6270, go north along the latter, through An-
gram, to Keld. There is a youth hostel at top Keld
which could act as a base. From Keld there are two
routes going south-east: one is the ancient Corpse
Way to Muker which leaves the dale and goes west
around Kisdon Hill; the other crosses the Swale where
it meets East Gill beck and follows an old lead ore
route via Crackpot Hall to Ivelet.

The first part of the Corpse Way is mostly firm and
stony and is easily followed between crumbling stone
walls. At the crest of Kisdon the way opens out and
the surface is a well-drained turf which is rideable.
The views across Swaledale from here are superb. The
descent to Muker is also firm and can be ridden.
Before Muker Church was built the nearest conse-
crated burial ground was at Grinton, a further 15
miles, and the old Corpse Way goes down across the
Swale to join the alternative route to Ivelet, and then
alongside the river eastwards.

The second route from Keld also climbs steeply
from the river and requires strenuous walking to
Crackpot Hall. The track then drops to follow the
river and the surface is a mixture of turf, sand and bog
according to location and the weather, but usually
firm enough for pleasant walking. At Holme Bridge
the Corpse Way is joined where it comes down from
Muker. A little further on, at Calvert House, the
surface becomes metalled. There are again two routes
from the next hamlet of Ivelet, with its humpbacked
bridge of 'Herriot' fame – it is said to be haunted by a
headless dog, which must, therefore, be fang-less –
the Corpse Way via Dyke Heads or the B6270 to
Gunnerside. Here again there are alternative routes:
the B6270 via Long Row, Feetham and Healaugh to
Reeth and Grinton, or a narrow lane to Crackpot
hamlet and either back on to the B6270 or across
Harkerside Moor to Grinton.

So, some stony steep rough stuff, some firm grassy rough stuff, and a clutter of alternative little lanes.

Background reading
James Herriot's *Yorkshire* (Michael Joseph, 1979) – spectacular photography.
Articles: Edward Grainger, 'In the Land of All Creatures', *Cycling* (15 November 1980).
Edward Grainger, 'Herriot Country', *Cycling World* (May 1982).
Albert Winstanley, 'Dale Road of the Dead', *Cycling World* (May 1982).
Albert Winstanley, 'Bitingly Cold, Misty and Green by the Swale', *Cycling* (17 February 1973).

Lancashire – Salters' Way

This has been chosen because it crosses the Forest of Bowland and can be used in conjunction with the North Lancashire Cycleway. The Salters' Way is about 15 miles long, crossing the forest diagonally from Hornby on the A683 (the nearest point on the Cycleway being Caton, 5 miles to the south) to Slaidburn where there is a convenient youth hostel.

Start at Hornby on the A683 coming south. The main road crosses the River Wenning and veers right, at which point the Salters' Way continues as a metalled lane crossing the minor (Wray) road. It climbs straightaway towards high moorland from which a number of rivers radiate, including the Hindburn, Roeburn and Hodder. Low gears will be needed but the surface is good. The road swoops to cross the Roeburn, then climbs again through Lower, Middle and High Salter where the metal ends and the aspect becomes more rugged and sparse.

There are excellent views, west to Morecambe Bay

and east to the Pennine chain. The Way rides high above the Roeburn for a couple of miles, and is a well-drained grass over grit track, but this depends on the season, then skirts Hawkshead, crossing feeder streams of the Roeburn before entering Salters' Fell where the going is rougher and stony. The bog is never far away and this difficult stretch can often lie water-logged.

After Salters' Fell comes Croasdale Fell and the brook which runs ahead to Slaidburn. The Way is steeply undulating, the surface reverting to gravel and becoming better drained. Then the road is metalled again and runs down to Slaidburn, and the North Lancashire Cycleway.

Much not-too-rugged rough stuff can be found along Forestry Commission tracks, the areas surrounding Water Authority reservoirs, and so on, where they are open to the public. The surfaces will vary from fine gravel to clay cushioned by pine needles, to crushed limestone. A whole network of lanes and tracks is to be found in Britain's forest parks.

Galloway Hills
Newton Stewart (A75/714) in the fine old county of Wigtownshire.

From Newton Stewart go north-west along the minor road which runs north of and parallel with the A714 and River Cree. After about 7 miles, shortly after crossing the Cree, turn right, then left at Stroan Bridge and right again on to the Straiton road. This follows the rapid-flowing Waters of Minnoch for several miles through Forestry Commission plantations with massive hills to the east, of which Merrick (2,764 feet) is the highest.

After about 8 miles of steady climbing the road

forks at Rowantree Toll, the right fork going to Straiton, and the left rising then descending fairly steeply for 3 miles to a bridge over the River Stinchar. (Take this left fork for an added loop of about 5 miles.) The descent, called Nick o' the Balloch, is animating but not terrifyingly steep, has a firm road surface but no road edges, and an unprotected drop to the left which means eyes on the road more than on the scenery unless going very slowly.

At Balloch, follow a forestry track, which goes east along the north bank of the Stinchar, to meet the metalled Glentrool to Straiton road which you had earlier forked from. Turn right, coming back south the short distance to Stinchar Bridge.

Here there is a Forestry Commission picnic site and other facilities. If you have the energy, ride up Salloch-on-Minnoch hill for a view of the rocky isle of Ailsa Craig, 10 miles out to sea, the coast itself being nearly 15 miles distant.

From Stinchar Bridge take a metalled road into Carrick Forest to the boomerang-shaped Loch Bradan. From here the track continues through fine forests to the shores of Loch Doon and its ruined castle. Turn left along the shore and soon the way becomes a good metalled road which takes you on to the A714 and into Dalmellington.

Then it is west, along 15 miles of moorland road, to Straiton, and south again to the start through Glen Trool.

Background reading: Maurice Teal, 'Gallivanting in Galloway', *Cycling* (15 September 1979);

John Buchan's *The Thirty-Nine Steps*, and follow the hero, Hannay, pedalling '. . . diligently up steep roads of hill gravel'.

There are, of course, similar networks of routes in the English New Forest and Forest of Dean; Snowdonia in Gwynedd (see also Railway Routes, p. 116);

and the Border, Queen Elizabeth, Glen More and Argyll forest parks in Scotland.

Old Railway Routes

Many new cycleways are being provided along the routes of old railways. The Derbyshire Manifold track has long been famous. It has, too, been infamous, because cycling has been allowed, banned, allowed again, and again banned, by successive bureaucratic edicts down the years. At present, largely owing to CTC pressure and local outcries, it is being allowed again, and hopefully for good.

A recent surge of official and environmental interest has been stimulated, largely by the Grimshaw plan. John Grimshaw & Associates (35 King Street, Bristol BS1 4DZ) have prepared a Government report suggesting the conversion of some 526 miles of railway lines into 800 miles of cycleways, thirty-three routes being specified.

Some of the longer routes are mentioned below, and their progress should be watched, though it is too much to hope that all will come to fruition. Even so, plans are well in hand for the development of some. For example, a 40-mile circuit of Birmingham, using old railway lines and canal paths, will soon be operational and will be called the 'Grimshaw Route' after its originator.

In Manchester, plans are well advanced for the conversion of the Accrington to Stockport and Macclesfield, via Manchester, line.

Perhaps the most encouraging cycleways provision is in Wales. In Gwynedd, a cycleway is to be built along the Welsh Highland track through the majestic Aberglaslyn Pass near Beddgelert, with two others planned for Snowdonia. Some old rail routes mooted for conversion are:

Corris to Machynlleth

(To digress: the latter is on Glyndwr's Way – *there's* some fine rough stuff for you to try. Go down to Plynlimon mountain via Glaslyn and find the sources of the rivers Wye and Severn.)

Betws-y-Coed to Bangor via Bethesda

Capel Curig to Betws-y-Coed

Carnarvon to Criccieth

Dolgellau to Penmaenpool

Beddgelert to Portmadoc

Carnarvon to Bangor

For further details of these Welsh routes contact: Gwynedd Cycleroutes, 372 High Street, Bangor.

For technical details of the following contact John Grimshaw & Associates; for progress on cycleroutes generally, as well as the conversion of railway lines, contact Friends of the Earth (London Headquarters).

Proposed Cycleways	*Total mileage of route*
1. Birmingham	39
2. Derby	20
3. Derbyshire – Peak District	39
4. Lancashire – Accrington to Macclesfield	52
5. Wales – Newport to Swansea	73
6. – Newport and Cwmbran, etc.	27
7. – Snowdonia	38
8. Cumbria – Keswick to Penrith	19
9. Yorks – Leeds to Wakefield and Barnsley	28
10. Durham – Newcastle to Durham and Barnard Castle	74
11. Hertfordshire	38
12. Nottingham'	16
13. Lancashire – Preston and Lancaster	20
14. Devon – Dartmoor – Plymouth to Princeton	17
15. Hampshire – New Forest	25

Canal Paths

Canal paths were hinted at above (Birmingham's Grimshaw Route) as being available for cycling. A timely article in *Bicycle Magazine* draws attention to the fact that the British Waterways Board issues a permit costing £1 which gives access to all the canal towpaths in Britain – even where local authorities put up 'no cycling' notices.

Canals go through the hearts of our greatest cities and across our finest countryside, built in one massive surge in a deliberate attempt to link the trading rivers – the Mersey, the Trent, the Thames, etc. – and can still give access to much traffic-free urban and rural scenery.

For permits, write to: The Canal Office, British Waterways Board, Delamere, Paddington, London W2 6ND ☎ 01-286 6101.

Background reading
See article, 'Exploring London's Canals by Bicycle', Nick Hanna, *Bicycle Magazine* (September 1982).
Also, if you can find it, 'Canal Capers down the Towpath', Albert Winstanley, *Cycling* (4 May 1974) which sees Albert along the Leeds and Liverpool Canal near Colne.

⑥

ROADCRAFT

It is a difficult business learning to ride a bike nowadays. In heavy traffic it can be unpleasant, frightening and dangerous. One great problem is that too many parents buy bicycles for their children, sending them on to the roads unaccompanied and untrained.

In this chapter on roadcraft and town cycling, I want first of all to make known the facilities for training children to ride cycles skilfully and safely, through RoSPA; then to give some specific advice for staying enjoyably awheel, based on my own experience.

The Royal Society for the Prevention of Accidents (RoSPA)

Most cyclists associate RoSPA with the National Cycling Proficiency Scheme (NCPS) and indeed the scheme continues to be a very important part of RoSPA's work in training young cyclists. However, the society has many other benefits for cyclists, and these will be described later.

The National Cycling Proficiency Scheme was the first planned effort, anywhere in the world, to shape the habits of road users by teaching them when they were young. It was launched as a joint scheme by RoSPA, the CTC and the (then) NCU, now BCF, in 1947, and has to date trained over four million young cyclists.

It is specifically designed for children aged nine to thirteen. The training course is short but intensive and practical, and its five or six sessions involve learning the Highway Code, basic roadcraft (cycle control, signalling, turning, etc.) and simple bicycle maintenance. Training is by local authority Road Safety Officers, teachers, the police, etc., both training and testing sessions being usually on school playgrounds or such places where road conditions can be simulated in safety.

In 1982, following intensive testing of materials, a new scheme was introduced by the society, called *Cycleway*. It is a classroom-based course lasting about a year, designed to harness children's interest in cycling. The course includes roadcraft training, projects, worksheets, etc., and involves the use of leaflets, booklets, slides, charts and other supporting materials. It comes in nine distinct units, the titles being:

Why ride a bicycle?
How does a bicycle work?
Communicating.
Why be prepared?
Starting to use the road.
Defensive cycling.
Getting used to the road.
Local conditions.
Course review.

RoSPA publishes a wide range of audio-visual material, which should be of value not only to teachers but to the many cycling clubs who take an interest in the training of their young members. These include safety and information posters, which should look good and be useful on school and club walls, such as:

Cycling as a sport,
Cyclist's map of Britain.

There are filmstrips and slides (and films – see Chapter 11) suitable for winter evening entertainment. There is a wide variety of leaflets, and the following books:

Bicycle Maintenance and Adjustment, 20pp. A clearly written and illustrated booklet, packed with information to help the cyclist maintain a roadworthy machine.

Cycle Sense, 16pp. Gives details of how both new and experienced cyclists can benefit by using the roads sensibly. It illustrates correct positioning for turns at junctions, roundabouts, etc., using full colour photographs.

Skilful Cycling, 36pp. Profusely illustrated guide to cycling and cycle maintenance, roadmanship, traffic signs, etc.

Another most useful publication is: *Report of the Working Party on Cycling Training for the Young* (October 1980).

The above, and many other facilities, are available from:

National Cycling Officer, RoSPA, Cannon House, The Priory Queensway, Birmingham B4 6BS ☎ 021-233 2461.

RoSPA, 41 South West Thistle Street Lane, Edinburgh EH2 1EW ☎ 031-226 6856.

RoSPA, 1st Floor, 1/3 Ty Glas Road, Llanishen, Cardiff ☎ 0222 762529.

RoSPA, 117 Lisburn Road, Belfast ☎ 0232 669453.

Some personal advice based on experience

OK Chris, it's great to hear that you're back on your bike after a break of several years. You did your RoSPA training at school but can only remember with

any clarity the advice to look out for car doors opening, and to wear bright clothes. *Come with me then* on
a ride along the High Street, and I'll try to get you to
the other end safely. We've checked your bike. Now
you need to remember the Highway Code, and ride
thoughtfully at all times.

Here's a good gap in the traffic. Let's move out.
Cycle a couple of feet out from the kerb. From now on
you'll have to look forward and around, taking stock
of the geography of the road, noting what is parked,
what is moving and how fast. Remember, because
motorists can't hear, they're almost blind – but you
can 'see' also with your ears. Use that advantage to
give yourself the room you need for safety.

Learn also to watch the road surface well ahead so
that you can decide early on any move. Grates pro-
trude into the road and you must move out in good
time.

You've been looking over your shoulder as often as
need be, keeping a watch on overtaking vehicles –
that's vital. You're judging their speed, size and
proximity by listening carefully. Note the engine tone.
It will tell you whether the vehicle is accelerating,
checking its speed because of you, revving impatiently
or in a cavalier manner.

A grate or any other smallish obstacle – even a
stone – must not loom up suddenly. If it does, you'll
either hit it and lose control or swerve without thinking and be hit by the lorry that's just going past.

There's another sort of obstacle ahead – have you
spotted it? A pot-hole. It's not against the kerb so you
can either go outside of it or inside. Remember, no
sudden swerving or acrobatics. If nothing is behind it
is safer to go outside – less grit and gravel, no chance
of clipping the kerb – but in continuous traffic you
must be prepared to go inside. If you are forced wide
though, and there is traffic about, you must give an

early and definite signal. This will give the traffic time
to adjust itself wide also.

Negotiated safely. Good thing you were alert early.

Hey! Be careful to keep a straight line at all times,
especially when looking over your shoulder. When you
get an opportunity, try this simple test on a deserted
road. Look over your right shoulder, turning your
head right round for a good look behind. Do this
several times. Notice that the bike turns right also –
towards the middle of the road. It's inevitable unless
compensated for. When the head turns, the trunk and
arms turn, the handlebars turn. When you've seen
how easy it is to swerve that critical yard that may take
you under the wheels of a car, practise keeping the
front wheel straight turning the arms left as the head
looks right. This exercise, perfected, could be a life
saver.

Good, you've noticed that the traffic's backing up
from a zebra crossing ahead and you've applied your
brakes to match your speed with it. It's perfectly legal
to overtake on the inside of slower-moving vehicles
but be careful for several reasons. The kerbside grates
and other obstacles will not be so easy to avoid; as you
ride more slowly it will be more difficult to maintain a
straight line and keep your balance; it will be easy to
catch your fingers or clothing on a protruding wing
mirror. Take my advice: never ride at speed down the
inside of stationary or slow-moving traffic. Not only is
it interpreted by motorists as a smug, provocative
gesture, it's a sure prelude to disaster – one day.
Pedestrians have a habit of nipping through lines of
cars and if you hit someone, even though it may not be
strictly your fault, you will feel utterly devastated and
miserable.

Keep your speed at about that of the traffic. If you
go faster, go slightly faster only. If the traffic has
stopped proceed slowly, under control, and alert.

The traffic's moving again now. Start slowly. No racing. Be prepared to stop again at the crossing.

You're zipping along quite fast now, in top gear. There are some traffic lights ahead, on green. The overtaking vehicles are accelerating, hoping to get across before the lights change. I can see that's in your mind too.

Ah! That's wise. You've eased off the pressure on the pedals and changed down a couple of gears, and I know why. At the zebra back there you found yourself in a high gear and had difficulty accelerating away. Car gears can be changed at a standstill, derailleur gears on a bike can't.

The lights have gone to amber, but you're ready to stop and to pull away again. You learn fast.

Here's another point though, and one that may save your life. It's especially important when the lights are at a cross-roads and you're waiting in company with a single vehicle, maybe a lorry. Other cars are being revved ready to turn to their right across your path. Never, *never* allow the vehicle you are waiting with to obscure you from their view. The best position is in line with the vehicle and well back from it so that the drivers of those other cars know that they cannot turn till both the lorry and you have gone over.

If you hang behind the lorry, and are obscured by it, as it pulls away it leaves you stranded and the other driver will be slamming into you before either of you are aware of it.

And another thing, *never* go alongside a lorry, or even what the car's indicators, position, speed, etc., all Try to predict what *all* close-by vehicles are going to do. Check on indicators, but don't rely on them. Make yourself visible to all drivers who pose a threat.

Too often a cyclist will go alongside a lorry which intends to turn left but has not signalled (and if the cyclist is already forward of the rear indicator how can he see anyway?) and the cyclist is then in danger of being dragged under the wheels as the vehicle turns across his path.

The lights have changed. Go across, but stop further along and I'll draw you a sketch to show you what I mean.

Now, we're in a busier part of town and lots of side streets meet the main road. Cars are constantly feeding on to the road and many come at speed to the junction before stopping suddenly.

It's disconcerting because you can never tell whether they will stop or simply drive out ignoring you. It's infuriating too. But, *always* be prepared to stop.

One effective way of stopping the motorist is to meet his eye. Look beyond the windscreen to the driver himself and tell him by your expression that you will be furious if he puts you in danger. Don't overdo it. Just look determined; a little stern. After a while you'll find that you can talk to drivers like this. Cyclists bother them because of the great variation in speed between one cyclist and another, variations which do not occur to such an extent with vehicles. In town, one cyclist can be doing 30 mph, another 5 mph. Not all motorists can cope mentally with that.

If there's one thing motorists hate, it's ditherers (not just cycling ditherers, but any sort) so they'll give you precedence and respect you if you show that you will not be pushed aside.

I reckon this is a good place to stop and talk about some general principles of behaviour. If you want to stay alive, treat all motorists as fools. In other words don't assume that they will do what they should, or even what the car's indicators, position, speed, etc., all suggest they will do. You, the cyclist, are vulnerable, not they. So, try both to anticipate what they will do and have the escape route/method planned in case they don't.

This is the sort of thing I mean. Suppose you're cycling along fairly briskly, as now. You see a car coming towards the junction ahead. You have the right of way but he's deadlier than an arrow and could be as merciless. You must think: suppose he shoots straight out, do I brake; do I swerve?

If he comes out, or even stops suddenly with his bonnet protruding across your path, the reaction would be to swerve outwards.

Have you already checked what is coming up behind? Is it safe to swerve? It may not be. You may avoid one and be smashed by another.

This is why, despite pride, it is vital to be mentally prepared to stop.

Despite my maxim: 'treat all motorists as fools', I've found that the majority are thoughtful and considerate. That is why I would advise: be alert, be forceful, but do not be aggressively defensive. It is much easier to manoeuvre a cycle than a car and the sensible rules of the sea are based on that principle. I have found that if I am courteous and considerate, being prepared to give way when sensible to do so, the tension between cyclist and motorist subsides.

So, keep good humoured, acknowledge with a wave of the hand, a nod of the head, and preferably a smile, any act of courtesy by a motorist. Your good manners will make the motorist more kindly disposed to the next cyclist he meets.

Never be rude. If a motorist nearly hits you or makes you swerve or check, show your displeasure (if you are *sure* he was 100 per cent to blame) by a resigned look, or a non-verbal 'tut-tut' by a throwing of the head. Then show him you'll forget it by giving him a withering look, followed by a shrug of the shoulders as if to say: 'Well, you're only a motorist;

what can one expect?' Such a sequence is more likely
to engender shame in the motorist, whereas outright
rudeness tends to produce an aggressive reaction.

After writing these cautions I saw a letter in
Cycling, part of which said:

'. . . I was forced into the kerb by a motorist to
which I responded, ill-advisedly as events trans-
pired, with an angry finger and fist gesticulation.

The driver stopped, got out and rummaged in
the boot, spinning round to face me with a large
monkey wrench held aloft and aimed at my head.
Fortunately I turned away taking a glancing blow to
the neck and shoulders.'

This type of incident, thankfully rare, illustrates
the antagonisms that cyclists may face, and reinforces
my contention that we need to cycle carefully and
courteously; not being pushed about, but not being
provocative.

In extreme cases be prepared to be angry, and show
it. If the motorist apologises be gracious and accept it,
then explain that your anger stems from real feelings
of danger and that people in charge of lethal machin-
ery should be careful, etc.

Always try to part in a friendly spirit. Nothing will
be gained by unappeased anger on either side.

Now, we're leaving the busy parts behind. Why not
have that burn-up you bought the bike for? Get a good
rhythm going, slip into top gear, increase speed.
Super. But don't be so absorbed in the thrill of the
wind and the hissing of the tyres that you forget the
road surface or the occasional car.

Ahead is a steep hill with a bend halfway down.
Don't go swooping down without putting both brakes
on a crack, so that they just engage the wheel.

Why?

Suppose you have to check suddenly. If the brakes
are slammed on from 'cold' you could be thrown over

the handlebars; yes, even by a back brake if it catches suddenly. If the brakes are already in position then just a little extra pressure is needed to bring them into operation.

The hill is very steep here. Sit well back on your saddle. Further back. As far back as you can, and lean your body back and down. This will minimise the forward momentum of your body and thus reduce the risk of being projected forward if you hit an obstacle.

Hmm. We're not out of trouble long. By chance we've hit this long straight stretch of road just as the local factory workers are changing shifts. Scores of cars are pouring out and in at speed. It's a two-lane road where cyclists are unwelcome because, like tractors, they slow the traffic and baulk overtaking.

You'll need to be very canny here. There's a line of cars coming towards you. If one pulls out and roars down the line he'll force you kerbwards as he squeezes through.

Now, some cyclists would move out from the kerb, occupying all of the left-hand carriageway. They argue that to do so forces motorists who might risk overtaking to hold back because the gap between cyclist and cars has been made too narrow.

If a motorist does try it, the cyclist can hold position till the last second, then swing back allowing himself more room than he would otherwise have been given.

It's a bit like Russian roulette though; especially if by studying the line of cars unceasingly, which you can't afford not to at this game, you have no chance to check what's coming up behind.

Don't do it. By all means keep out an extra foot. To squeeze yourself up against the kerb is asking to be swept aside. But don't let that devil pride leave you stranded in the middle of the road like a turkey on a motorway. You may think you can force the traffic to do what you want. Ultimately you can't. Be wrong – you're dead.

And talking about pride, let's give it a drubbing along here.

We're going to make one of the most dangerous moves on two wheels. Turning right. I know you won't like it, few cyclists do, but it's sometimes prudent to do so – stopping on the left and waiting till the road is clear before going across.

Yes, I know it feels like cowardice, but I suspect it's less painful than having a juggernaut pulp your foot or a surgeon take spokes out of your thigh. If you do turn right across the traffic, which experienced cyclists invariably do without fear or jeopardy, and you have to wait on the crown of the road, put a foot down close to the machine to steady yourself. Don't try a balancing act. It looks impressive just prior to the fall that makes you look a fool.

I noticed you jump when that car overtook you too close, too fast. This is another situation which some cyclists try to avoid by forcing cars to slow down or wait behind. It's similar to the tactic above which I warned against – moving out into the road to baulk the traffic. It's very dangerous to try to slow down to 18 mph something that's been doing about 60 mph. It infuriates the motorist if it's done blatantly and could goad some drivers into reprisals they might not otherwise consider.

Let me try to describe a couple of more positive ways of maintaining the amount of road a cyclist has a right to, for his own safety and comfort.

Suppose a vehicle is approaching from behind and in your experience there is very little room for it to overtake at speed. So, you don't begrudge the vehicle coming past, but you want to be sure it's giving you a wide berth. In that case, take your right hand from the handlebars and drop your hand deliberately by your side. Now, according to the amount of space you need tilt up your hand.

If you want a fair amount of room, show it by raising the arm slightly, to, say, thirty degrees from the vertical, but no further in case it's mistaken for a feeble turning-right signal.

If you want the vehicle to slow down and wait behind you, drop your arm as before but open your hand to face the vehicle driver. At the same time look over your right shoulder to reinforce the signal.

This is specially useful if you are being followed towards a left-hand bend by a vehicle and, because you are ahead, you know that another vehicle or other hazard is there. The driver behind may be tempted to overtake by swinging round you. He could then only avoid disaster to himself by inflicting it on you as he squeezes back in.

These communications then, deliberately and clearly given, can be your means of controlling following vehicles for mutual benefit. I have almost always found them effective, and motorist friends who have seen me use them say that the message is unmistakable.

One final point on courtesy. Always acknowledge a driver who has responded to these or other signals. If possible, raise your hand as he goes past. I think you'll find that many motorists will acknowledge this gesture and the road must be a safer place following such mutual respect.

7

THE CYCLE
Keeping it in Good Order

It is regrettable that many cycles are sold by multiple stores and non-specialist shops which provide no repair or after sales service. It is not only regrettable – it is deplorable.

What motorist would tolerate a garage which sold him a car and then refused to service or repair it, or replace all or any parts of it if need be?

Few cyclists can cope with all problems that arise and ought to be able to take the machine to a local reputable repairer. I would advise all cyclists, where it is possible, to support fully any cycle dealer who repairs bikes as well. There are bigger profits in selling bikes than in repairing them and a shop which puts itself out for customers by attending to all sorts of technical repairs deserves respect and custom. (See 'Association of Cycle Traders', Chapter 1.)

Let me suppose that the average cyclist will want to do most repairs himself. Fine. Yet there are some jobs which, with the proper training and equipment, take ten minutes, but will have the average cyclist struggling for a day or more. So I would say, unless you have an engineering background, special skill or interest, and good repair facilities, tackle the small jobs yourself and leave the bigger ones for an expert. And do not begrudge his charges.

Examples: almost anyone can replace a single snapped spoke but few can true or rebuild a wheel; with a block remover and a good vice a block can be taken off a wheel in a few seconds, but without these the job is well nigh impossible; a chain can be split and shortened in a few minutes with a rivet remover but it is very tricky getting the rivet back in, and it is galling to have the chain come apart an hour later 5 miles down the road.

So, do not be ashamed to admit that some jobs are best handed over to others. The last thing we need on the road is a badly repaired cycle.

Repairs can be reduced to a minimum if:

(a) the cycle is kept clean,
(b) moving parts are regularly lubricated,
(c) a check is kept on wear and tear.

A clean bike is not merely aesthetically pleasing and good to ride, it is the prime condition for efficiency. The dark winter days with snow, ice and salt on commuter roads make a perpetually clean cycle impossible, but there should be time to take away the worst of the grime. The frame should be cleaned with soap and water, any swarf being removed with strips of paraffined cloth. The latter should also be used to remove grime from wheel axles, pedals, and the bottom bracket. The chain, back sprockets and rollers of derailleur gears will soon become caked in a gritty black deposit. Unless this is scraped away regularly it searches out bearings and causes wear; this is soon followed by a noticeable 'play' in moving parts and rapid failure.

While cleaning the bike, check the tread of the tyres for any occluded grit or glass which will ultimately break through and cause a puncture.

Lubrication is vital. A couple of days of snow and salt can leach every bit of grease out of a chain, leaving it dry and rusty. Check all moving parts at least once a week. Having cleaned the machine thoroughly, apply oil to wheel spindles, brake arms, pedals, bottom bracket, freewheel, gear rollers, and all exposed cables of brakes and gears, working it in by keeping the parts moving. But be sure to remove all excess oil with a clean cloth because it acts as a collector of dirt.

Oil can also be put into brake cable housings at both ends by up-ending the bike and draining it in mechanically. This is a slow job because care must be taken to use only small amounts efficiently, wiping away excess, but I have found it a sure way to avoid brake failure and cable breakages. It is possible to buy spray lubricants for such tricky areas; these are less messy but less efficient.

The chain should be oiled regularly after cleaning, and the excess removed. Every half year or less, according to usage, it should be greased. I have found the following method reliable: drop out the rear wheel to leave the chain loose but intact; clean it thoroughly with a petrol rag; having bought some graphite grease, melt it in a shallow tray and while still hot immerse sections of the chain in turn for several minutes; when cool, clean away surface grease.

Cleaned chains can be protected using silicone-based sprays.

Attend to details. For example, unscrew and grease regularly the screws and bolts of mudguards; also the bolts of brake cable anchors, brake blocks, and panniers, etc. Loosen off, grease and tighten pedals, cranks, bottom bracket, headset, handlebars and saddle bolts. One cold stormy night you may be grateful for such prudence.

Check for wear and tear. Tyres should be inflated to recommended pressures because soft tyres suffer from wall cracking and collapse. Watch for tyre wear; all but heavy duty roadster tyres have a lamentably short life, especially on winter grit. I would urge riders to carry spare inner tubes to replace punctured ones – repair these later. Butyl tubes cannot be mended quickly. I have found the following to be a reliable procedure: clean the area around the puncture with grease solvent (petrol, meths); put on repair solution; wait half an hour till perfectly dry; apply a second coating, and wait about 5 minutes; place patch over and firm down; chalk the surrounding area to prevent sticking.

Always replace the inner tube fully deflated. Make sure the tube at the valve is pushed fully into the tyre and the latter seated on to the rim properly. If possible, prise the tyre back on with the fingers, avoiding the use of levers which can so easily pinch another hole in the tube.

Check brake block wear. Adjust the cable when necessary. This is best done with two pairs of hands but a single pair – determined – can succeed. To do this: release the cable anchor bolt with a pair of pliers; squeeze the yokes (arms) of the brake; pull the cable to full tension and tighten the cable anchor bolt. Easily described; in fact, quite tricky.

Check for sloppiness, especially of the bottom bracket. Where necessary, loosen the locking ring using gentle hammer taps on a wooden-handled screwdriver, and gradually tighten the adjustable cup using a hammer and centre punch (or 5-inch nail) in the holes provided. Re-tighten the locking ring.

Creaking noises when pedalling could be due to dryness or rust in the pedals, but persistent clicks probably mean a broken ball bearing in pedal or bottom bracket.

I have found that the above procedures, available even to the non-technical cyclist who lives in a high rise flat, can reduce mechanical failure to an acceptable minimum.

Those who want to tackle every job on the machine, including more specialised tasks, such as repairing and fitting tubular tyres, will probably already be members of cycle clubs where expertise can be picked up from experienced cyclists. Some larger urban clubs arrange cycle repair workshops, and both the British Cycling Coaching Scheme and some FoE groups, mentioned elsewhere, include training workshops in their programmes. All the cycling press carry regular features on equipment, and excellent manuals now exist (see Books, Chapter 11) to help the DIY enthusiast.

8
THE CYCLE AND CYCLISTS
Its Equipment, and Theirs

The range of cycling equipment is now so wide, catering for everything from small-wheeled BMX machines to tandem racers, that a comprehensive survey would require a whole book. In fact, the best ways to educate oneself are either to visit a large cycle shop and browse, or to send for some of the mail order catalogues advertised in the cycling press.

A brief look then at basic equipment, bearing in mind that so much depends upon:

    (a) what the bike is being used for (touring, racing, commuting, rough stuff, knockabout . . .),

    (b) preferences (frame angles, type and number of gears, shape and set of handlebars . . .),

    (c) the money available (no small consideration).

The quality of a machine clearly resides in (c). Good touring bikes and their accessories are as expensive as racing cycles, and BMX, cyclo-cross, tricycle, tandem machines, etc., all have their top-of-the-range prices.

It is difficult to give advice, other than the effete: 'buy the best you can afford'. Yet it is true. Whatever the type of bike, it is far better to save a little longer and buy a frame with Reynolds 531 tubing, because it will give reliable service for years. With accessories too, the same applies. A cheap, off-the-peg machine will gleam in the shop window, but who wants rusty cranks six wet weeks later? I have found that I cannot afford to keep buying cheap bikes or parts – ultimately, the best quality is cheapest.

Arguments rage as to which type of equipment is 'best'. For example, brakes. Do you have hub, or disc, or calliper? If calliper, do you have cantilever, side- or centre-pull? Experts debate in print about suitability, efficiency, performance; quoting research findings, stopping distances, etc. All fascinating stuff. In the end it often happens that you get used to the first sort you buy and go on buying it when a replacement is necessary; or you have a bad experience of a bike or part, and never buy one again.

Having said that it is well nigh impossible in so short a space to describe, and unwise in so broad an area to pontificate, let me give some thoughts based on experience, which should help.

I have already mentioned the frame. Get Reynolds 531 double butted and lugged tubing if you can afford it. It will last a lifetime. The size and angles will depend on the rider's height and the purpose of the machine. Angles affect only racing cyclists, especially bikers and their track machines, and need not concern the ordinary rider. I would say, always have racing handlebars since these afford several grip positions and are more comfortable. If they are not well taped, put some on. There are several types of tapes, from thin plastic to cushioned foam, and you will soon find your favourite.

I have always found centre-pull brakes best. I have disc brakes on both a tricycle and a tandem but have never been very impressed by their efficiency. The disc is the legally required second brake on the trike, but two independent front callipers could be fitted. If you are offered brakes with a second touring lever, to be operated when riding 'on the tops' – decline them. I have used them but find the second levers cumbersome and unnecessary. Perhaps I have not persevered enough.

For me there is no substitute for derailleur gears

and I have used Campagnolo equipment for many years. Other types, and makes, give good performance in relation to their cost. Some cyclists prefer other gears, for example Sturmey-Archer, and I suspect they are equally pleased with the performance they get. I reckon these days, with the ability of parallelogram gears to cope with wide variations in sprocket size, there is no real need for double chain wheels. If you want ten or twelve gears, especially for low gearing with loads up long hills whilst touring, fine. But if you rarely meet considerable hills, a single chainwheel of forty-eight teeth will prove far less trouble, and, with sprockets ranging from thirteen to twenty-eight teeth, will give gears capable of dealing with most slopes. If not, walk a few yards.

There is, of course, the fixed gear. I have a fixed cog machine (chainwheel forty-six: sprocket seventeen) which I use on icy or snowy roads. The reckoning is that the steady pedalling improves road holding and the fixed cog gives an extra brake, and indeed can be used instead of a brake where this might create a skid. In truth, there are times, on the steep hills near home, when it terrifies me. It is superb though on level roads in urban areas where steady but rapid acceleration and braking are constantly needed.

Toeclips are essential. There are some cyclists who do not like to be taken for enthusiasts or racing cyclists, and who shun toeclips for that reason. Others fear they will be trapped in and prefer to put their feet down unhindered and easily when coming to a stop. They also suspect they will look foolish trying to flick the pedals into position as they ride away again. In fact, it takes just a few hours to gain enough skill to cope, and after a few days it becomes second nature. The benefits, chiefly in giving extra thrust and preventing slip, make them invaluable.

Use rat trap pedals, but get them wide enough.

Wheels can be chosen according to preference, whether steel or alloy, whether with conventional nuts or quick release. But if you have the latter, carry a long-wired anti-thief device and thread it through the wheels as well as the frame. Tyres, again, come by choice, with certain exceptions. For example, some lightweight touring cycles have very little clearance between the chain stays and the wheel, in which case a narrow gauge lightweight tyre or tube must be used. A long distance tourist who prefers a rugged back tyre must be aware of this when ordering or buying a frame.

Cranks with cotter pins are on the way out. One problem of the current trend towards cotterless cranks and other innovations seems to be the need to provide oneself with a multitude of tools. Not only are Allen keys essential now, but the new sizes of nuts and bolts almost fit every spanner – so the spanner either does not quite go over the nut, or seems to fit and then slips at the last moment. What can be blamed? Metrication? The Japanese? Where is the standardisation that EEC membership was supposed to bring? Those must have been simple halcyon days when a single BSA spanner fitted every nut on the bike.

What tools you buy, depends on the jobs you want to do, but touring cyclists will need to carry screw-drivers, a selection of spanners, tyre levers, small pliers, copper wire, scissors, string and tape. Carry all tools, all loads, in saddlebag or panniers; never on the person.

Saddle? Certainly. Comfort will decide. If you select a porous type carry a plastic bag to cover it if left in the rain. Or splash out on a saddle cover.

Mudguards? Yes. Two. Full length.

A pump should always be carried, and carried away if the cycle is parked. Never cycle without a substantial lock and wire (the 'uncuttable with wire cutters' type) and long enough to secure the machine to a lamp post, drainpipe, etc.

I reckon a bell, of the ping variety, to be vital. It does not make a lot of noise but it says 'bicycle' to the person just stepping off the kerb. A shout is no good under such circumstances.

For the three months or so of commuter darkness, 20 miles a day, I prefer battery lights. I carry spare bulbs which are rarely needed, and change the batteries regularly so as to have bright lights at all times. It is no good just to be legal; one must be seen. All cycle lights can be temperamental and a rogue lamp is infuriating. If in doubt about a lamp's reliability, fit two rear ones so as to guarantee that one is always on. It is not expensive where life depends on it. I have tried various types of dynamo lighting over the years but find them disadvantageous for various reasons, including:

(a) slowing the bike and creating more work,
(b) the wiring etc. makes more grot accumulate in bad weather,
(c) it is susceptible to damp,
(d) it cannot easily be put on or taken off at whim.

For those who like them, and for those who like experimenting with personalised circuits, rechargeable batteries, etc., the subject gets plenty of airing in the cycling papers.

As far as clothing is concerned, it is an area which is even more susceptible to personal preference. Some people are swayed by fashion; club cyclists, for example, when riding with the club. Otherwise it becomes a personal thing: 'I wouldn't be seen dead in . . .'.

So, whether it is to be shorts, or bags, or plusses, or track suits, or lounge suits, is neither here nor there. If the weather is cold, the clothing must keep you warm; if hot, cool; if wet, dry. There are, however, some general points that must be made.

Most cyclists under-dress when inexperienced, and not only in cold weather. Try this test. Select the hottest day in high summer and go for a 10-mile ride stripped to the waist (or, I should say, with shoulders bare!). When you get home put your hands on your neck and shoulders. They will be hot to the point of soreness. Now touch your stomach. It will be ice cold. Therefore always wear a cool, loose-fitting sweatshirt in unremitting sun because the wind cuts out none of the radiation which causes sunburn and sunstroke. The stomach gets all the buffeting of the air and is not generating its own movement heat. Bear this in mind in the winter and keep well wrapped in woollies which will also protect the kidneys and help to prevent back trouble.

Always carry extra clothing if you can, even if sometimes you do not use it.

Keeping dry is essential, especially on distance tours. Capes and leggings are still popular but rain-suits made of waterproof breathable fabric are increasing in efficiency and use. They are, however, expensive. Capes make one sweat underneath less than leggings but are difficult in wind and when riding amongst juggernauts. I have found a pair of light, not-quite waterproof but windproof over-trousers to be the best ally of a cape in light rain, and they are superb as an extra skin during bitter weather. They have another value; being easily washed and dried they keep any undergear free from salt spray and grime.

Shoes. I cannot think that any serious cyclist would pedal off without specialist cycling shoes, racing, or touring type with a heel. Made of supple leather they are comfortable, durable and brought up like new, even after prolonged exposure to rain or snow, if dried slowly and polished. The soles are usually too thin for my liking and I fix a rubber stick-on sole. On only one pair did I put metal plates, but I found walking ungainly, idiotic. The plates have their uses, but the plain shoes plus toeclips serve all my purposes.

Much more could be said, but a final comment only: you know yourself better than anyone else does. So, if you suffer from ear-ache, wear a balaclava; if you get knee pains in cold weather, wear long johns; if you are prone to a bad back, wear braces and long jackets. In other words, though the clothing may not be fashionable cycling gear, if you need it, wear it. Ultimately it does not matter what you look like, but how you feel. Feel good, and you will be able to cycle on and on and . . .

9

CYCLING HOLIDAYS

The variety of types of cycling holiday is very wide. For simplicity they may be grouped under three headings:

    (a) Home-based tours.
    (b) Riding further afield.
    (c) Organised fixed-centre holidays and tours.

Home-based Tours

Few cyclists have not started their cycling careers with plenty of forays, a few hours at a stretch, in the area around their home. This is the finest introduction to excursions further afield. Indeed, many thoroughly grounded cycle tourists have an unashamed pride in their knowledge of their own locality.

The first great advantage of the home-based tour is the ability to travel light. The amount and sort of clothing can be gauged very accurately from day to day. If, by chance, a mistake is made and the weather becomes foul, one can head for home after only a moment's thought.

There are two disadvantages to be aware of. Heading for home is the sort of cowardice no self-respecting cyclist will take pleasure in. On the other hand, it is easy to set off with enormous enthusiasm and a following wind, sail too far out, and have to contend with a strength-sapping wind all the long way home.

The best idea is to plan short circular routes,

expanding the circle as confidence and experience grow. Within a short time all the gradients, dangerous bends, windswept hill-tops, dragstrips of main roads, narrow country lanes, etc., will be well known.

A cyclist must have knowledge of three things: himself, his cycle and the road beneath. Once he is sure of his own ability, is confident of the trust he can put in his machine, and knows the locality, he can begin the satisfying business of cycle touring; he can begin the in-depth exploration of the area around.

The cyclist can simply set off, to see what comes along, to revel in the sounds, smells, sights and happenings along the way, to be thrilled by just being out there. He is likely to be more satisfied though, and to experience more, if he goes prepared. He should have a theme, an objective. Ideas are legion. Guide books and local history books and maps will be sure to spark off enthusiasms. The local library, especially if it doubles as a centre for the local Tourist Board, will have pamphlets, leaflets, booklets galore, to feed the imagination.

The Tourist Boards publish guidebooks giving information on:

Historic Houses, Castles and Gardens
Museums and Art Galleries
Animal and Wildlife Parks
Country Parks, Amusement and Water Parks
Windmills and Watermills
Caves and Mines
Steam, Miniature and Model Railways
Stone Circles
Churches and Cathedrals
Canals, Rivers, Lakes, Reservoirs, etc.
Contact:
English Tourist Board, 4 Grosvenor Gardens, London SW1 ☎ 01-730 3400.

Northern Ireland Tourist Board, 48 High Street, Belfast ☎ 0232 31221.

Scottish Tourist Board, 23 Ravelston Terrace, Edinburgh 4 ☎ 031-332 2433.

Wales Tourist Board, Welcome House, High Street, Llandaff ☎ Cardiff 0222 567701.

In addition, information will be found about the properties open to the public which are owned by the National Trust and the Department of the Environment.

Contact:

The National Trust, 40–42 Queen Anne's Gate, Westminster SW1 ☎ 01-222 9251.

Department of the Environment, 2 Marsham Street, London SW1 ☎ 01-212 3434.

Apart from these formal venues there is the enjoyment to be gained from getting to know the towns and villages in the neighbourhood. Literally hundreds of these will lie within a radius of 20 miles from the home of most people in Britain. It will be possible, with a little experience, to discover the old village forge, or bakehouse, school, winnowing barn, or pub, all of which may have been converted into private homes. Looking more closely you may be able to find village pumps, dovecotes, the market cross, perhaps a pillory or stocks, and so on. There are few places without something unusual. You could follow a theme through, for example:

visit all the nearby reservoirs;

follow a brook, canal or river as far as you can;

follow a road, track or bridleway, etc.

Here is just one theme to exhaust: Horse Shoes. Find and visit all the pubs in the locality with horse shoes in the name; visit collections of horse shoes, as at Scarrington, near Bingham; visit the brick horse shoe at Gonalston, south of Southwell; visit Oakham Castle with its unique collection of horse shoes; visit buildings, usually former forges, with horse shoe decorations; etc. A collection of slides, based on an idea like this, would provide a fascinating slide show for a cycle club evening.

Cycling Further Afield

There are many places just beyond a day's cycle ride away that cyclists will want to visit. This means staying away overnight, and there are several ways of doing this which may be chosen by preference or pocket. These include:

Hostelling

Bed-and-Breakfast – Guest House/Hotel/Farm-house, etc.

Camping

In this section of the chapter each of these will be considered in some depth.

The Youth Hostels Association

The provision of a hostel network has enabled cyclists to ride far from home at very reasonable cost.

Most people know a little about the YHA and only a brief comment need be added here to put things in perspective. It is an organisation to help the young, and those of limited means, to enjoy the countryside by providing accommodation at as low a cost as possible. There are over 250 hostels in England and Wales, and about 100 more in Scotland and Northern Ireland.

Membership of the YHA enables the member to stay in any hostel in that calendar year, to receive the handbook and the quarterly newspaper, *Hostelling News*, and to join the local YHA group.

The handbook gives full information about membership, bookings, regulations and charges, plus general advice and details about every hostel.

These are some examples of specific facilities for cyclists:

Border and Dales
Cycles for hire – small returnable deposit required – at Barnard Castle and Grinton Lodge, both about 10 miles from Darlington.

Eastern
Cycle hire is available at Blaxhall, Brandon, Castle Hedingham, Great Yarmouth, Hunstanton, Nedging Tye and Sheringham. Inclusive holidays are arranged with cycle hire and accommodation at hostels. (Enquiries to: East Anglian Cycling Holidays, Holly Tree Farm, Yoxford, Suffolk.)

Isle of Wight
Cycles may be hired at Whitwell.

Lakeland
Some local firms operate a cycle hire scheme. (Stamped addressed envelope to YHA regional office, Elleray, Windermere, Cumbria LA23 1AW, for details.)

Midland
'Hub of England Cycle Hire' is now well established, being originally launched with help from the Countryside Commission. It is run from the hostels at Badby, Charlbury, Duntisbourne Abbotts and Greens Norton, and is ideal for Northamptonshire and the Cotswolds. Cyclists may go where they please, but at least one night must be spent at a hostel and the cycle must be returned to the hostel it came from. Detailed routes and maps have been prepared by the CTC. (A leaflet and booking form may be obtained from:

Hub of England Cycle Hire, YHA, 116 Birmingham Road, Lichfield, Staffordshire WS14 9BW; stamped addressed envelope required.)

Peak
This region operates an inter-hostel cycle scheme. A number of routes are available. (Stamped addressed envelope to Crompton Chambers, 55 Dale Road, Matlock, Derbyshire DE4 3LT.)

Cycle hire is available at several other centres locally (see Cycle Hire).

South Wales
Cycle hire at St Athan Youth Hostel.

South-west
Cycles may be hired at Bath, Bridport, Land's End, Tavistock and Treyarnon Bay.

Southern
Cycles may be hired, subject to availability, at Beachy Head, Streatley-on-Thames, Truleigh Hill and Winchester.

Yorkshire
Cycles may be hired at Malton. This is particularly useful as there is a family cottage with garage next to the hostel.

Thus, the cyclist may either use his own cycle, staying at hostels along the way, or he may arrive at a hostel by public transport or car, and hire a cycle for short or extended tours according to the facilities available.

Full details of all facilities available to cyclists at hostels may be obtained from the national organisation at the addresses below.

Youth Hostels Association (England and Wales), Trevelyan House, 8 St Stephen's Hill, St Albans AL1 2DY ☎ 0727 55215.

Scottish Youth Hostels Association, 7 Glebe Crescent, Stirling FK8 2JA.

Youth Hostel Association of Northern Ireland, 56 Bradbury Place, Belfast, Northern Ireland ☎ Belfast 24733.

Hostels for fixed-centre and family accommodation

The idea of being perpetually on the move does not appeal to all cyclists, nor is it always convenient. The area around any particular hostel may be so full of interest that several days will be needed for it to be explored to satisfaction.

Families, particularly, will find 'living out of a saddlebag' unnecessarily harassing. For these and other reasons the YHA has progressed from the stay-a-night-and-move-on principle to three consecutive nights' stay in a hostel and, if the hostel is not too busy, extending beyond this at the discretion of the warden.

Many hostels (twenty-three in England and Wales) have accommodation where a family can be self-contained and (sometimes) entirely private. The family is allowed to stay one full week, Saturday to Saturday; the only condition for eligibility is that at least one child must be under five years of age.

Facilities are excellent but varied. At Malton, north of York, the family stay in a large separate cottage; at Castle Hedingham, near Braintree in Essex, purpose-built accommodation is shared by two families (separate bedrooms but one kitchen and dining room).

Where such family accommodation coincides with

cycle hire, as in the two examples quoted, the family may travel to the hostel by car or public transport and then spend the week exploring the locality awheel. Because the usual requirement to be out of the hostel during the day is waived, the family need not fear the weather. If it is very wet they can stay in; if they get wet they can come in. This liberal regime is a superb encouragement to parents to keep hostelling and cycling when their children are very young.

In some regions, families are allowed to use part of a hostel if it is not too busy. This is entirely at the discretion of the warden. It is worth enquiring about when a hostel route is being planned. Again, some hostels have family rooms. Cyclists are gregarious; so are cycling families. By seeking out and using separate facilities the cycling family has no intention of segregating itself. Parents find it easier to relax and deal with the minutiae of family life if they can do it without being a nuisance to others. When the essential commitment has been discharged, the family may take part fully in the life of the hostel.

Cyclists will have many reasons for wanting to use a hostel as a fixed centre. Many will cycle to hostels which offer, or are close to, special facilities – rock climbing, mountain walking, pony trekking, canoeing, all forms of local and natural history. Most cyclists, however, will want to use their cycles most if not all of the time – to some cyclists, it is unthinkable to be without the cycle.

For these, the freedom of the roads exists in all directions from the hostel. They may, however, take advantage of special cycling weeks arranged at some hostels. A recent innovation at Westerdale hostel was a 'Bring a Bike' scheme of two weekends in this 'grand old shooting lodge set in the heart of the North Yorkshire Moors National Park amidst peaceful scenery and quiet country lanes'. The area is further described as having 'suitable roads and tracks for cycling, and nearby is the famous Rosedale Chimney which has proved a challenge for many an experienced cyclist!' The weekends were designed for both experienced and novice riders, with graded routes varying from 20 to 50 miles a day. The evenings were given over to informal talks on cycling, modern cycles and equipment. One of the great advantages of such introductory weekends is that most participants will be from the immediate locality. Their knowledge of the area will be immense and will act as a superb initiation to the locality for the hosteller from further afield. Such a weekend could act as a stimulus to use the hostel for a fixed centre with more freedom to continue the exploration.

Another example of two introductory weekends was the invitation from Hartington hostel near Buxton in Derbyshire. The weekends included such organised extras as walking, cycling and film shows. The participants did not have to be YHA members – a useful non-obligatory beginning on which to build more adventurous excursions.

A novel idea, tried by the CTC, was a 'teach-in', spanning four days, for twelve to twenty year olds. The CTC asked the question: 'How do you teach youngsters about cycle touring?' and came up with the answer: 'Take them to a pleasant and uncrowded corner of the country, make sure they know how to look after their bikes, show them how to use a map, and then – go cycling.'

They went to Knighton hostel in mid Wales. The group worked hard. They watched slides and film shows, demonstrations of cycle maintenance and repair, with plenty of practice, were shown how to read a map, and then went riding. The course ended with the leader trying to ford a stream on a tricycle, giving up when the water reached the saddle.

This pilot scheme is to be developed further with the cooperation of RoSPA and schools. The CTC will supply details to anyone interested.

Guest Houses, Farmhouses, Hotels . . .

A significant number of cyclists wish to ride alone, in pairs or very small groups. They do not relish being organised. The cycle has freed them and they have no wish but to follow their own impromptu desires. Many cyclists plan routes in great detail and promptly abandon the schedule when the wheels touch the road; they had their fun planning, but even plans can be a straitjacket and to throw them aside has a pleasure all of its own. Many more cyclists set off having only the haziest of directional plans in mind. 'I'll turn right out of the gate and head roughly north towards the Lake District.' Thereafter they could end up . . .?

Such riders have only the basic questions in mind: where shall I eat during the day, and where shall I spend the night? They begin to look for a cafe or restaurant about half-an-hour before 'hunger knocks', and they begin thinking about accommodation at any time between 3 and 9 p.m., depending on the area or time of year.

Cyclists of this variety, with many years of experience, will have taken a vital precaution. If they have not already phoned ahead to book accommodation they will have handbooks or accommodation guides stowed away in the side pockets of saddlebag or panniers. The handbooks will probably have small pieces of paper tucked in – addresses from cycling newspapers and magazines which they have saved in readiness for such an excursion.

One vital point must be made at this stage: cyclists will be sure to find a welcome at accommodation advertised in cycling publications. The same guaran-

tee cannot be given of hotels or guest houses dis-
covered by chance or advertised elsewhere. It is a
lesson often hard-earned. Those owners, managers or
landladies who specifically encourage cyclists to stay
know how to look after them. They have the patience
to cope with drenched capes and sodden socks, will
provide drying facilities, secure shelter for the bikes,
steaming tea and plenty of filling food. There can be
few things worse than booking in for the night, finding
all sorts of obstacles to comfort, a grudging provision
of basic needs, and finally admitting that it was all a
mistake.

Addresses for accommodation and advertisements
which appear in the CTC handbook, and other publications of that sort, have been used by cyclists, in
some cases, for decades. They have a seal of approval
based on long and happy association with cyclists and
indeed often appear in print in the cycling press by
direct recommendation from satisfied cyclists.

A serious caution must be included. The freedom
referred to earlier, to leave decisions of accommodation to the last minute, can become irresponsible and
thoughtless, leading to cyclists getting a bad name.
Cyclists should by all means be free to wander but
ought not to put other people under pressure *if it can
be avoided.* It is best to give hotel or guest house
owners as much notice as possible, by booking, if the
day's venue is known, or by phoning ahead, and by
stating and keeping to the time of arrival.

Experience shows, sadly, that the cyclist has to
work harder than almost any other member of the
travelling public to be accepted amicably in such
establishments as public houses, hotels and guest
houses. Happily, where the cyclist has shown himself
to be reasonable, good-tempered and good-
humoured, he wins respect not only for himself but for
cyclists generally.

If the guest house, farmhouse, hotel, etc., were seen just as a freer but more expensive hostel, all would have been said. However, more and more such establishments are beginning to cater specifically for cyclists and many sorts of opportunities now exist for different types of holidays (see Fixed-Centre Holidays and Tours).

NB Full lists of guest houses, etc., appear in the CTC handbook, and there are advertisement columns in *Cycletouring* magazine, and in other cycling journals.

Cycle Camping

Camping provides real freedom, both for the individual and for groups. Before going into detail, two points must be made:

(a) it provides freedom of movement only to those who have prepared for it properly,

(b) it is not cheap, only comparatively so, and indeed the initial outlay for good equipment can be considerable.

The best preparation for the total novice should be background reading and club membership, but I will return to these later.

The keen bikepacker will have some basic considerations:

(i) How to choose the best cycle and accessories.

(ii) How to select only essential equipment, eliminating superfluous items.

(iii) How to match lightness of equipment with both performance and cost.

(iv) How to load the machine.

(v) Where to camp.

The first essential is a strong and reliable cycle. The combined weight of rider and loaded panniers may be over 200 lb (91 kg) and a machine carrying that load for mile after mile will take some punishment. A cycle with double butted Reynolds 531 tubing should be sought, lightweight if preferred, but touring not racing frame, with steel (not alloy) wheels. Steel is much stronger but has the disadvantage of poorer braking performance and a heavily laden machine going down a steep winding hill in pouring rain can create excitement best avoided. Therefore select brake-blocks for steel wheels (leather blocks such as Fibrax Raincheater or Raleigh Raincheck – *never* rubber) remembering to change them whenever you change steel for alloy or vice versa.

Fit good-sized rear and front wheel panniers, as low down as practicable so as to lower the centre of gravity and maximise balance and control. Even weight distribution around front and rear wheels helps to stabilise the whole machine and, though it may look cumbersome, makes for easier handling than a cycle with all the weight at the back. It will also reduce the risk of rear wheel spoke breakages.

Always use racing handlebars which give several grip positions. If you ride a laden straight barred machine for several hours you will have numbed and tingling fingers for several days.

Heavily laden cycle tourists need to give extra care to accessories. For example, make sure that neither front nor rear lamps are obscured by any of the luggage. Fit a reliable bell. Fit a mirror, for without it an over-the-shoulder glance could start a wobble that is impossible to correct. But do not rely entirely on the mirror: use it in addition to looking, or instead – on tricky descents for example.

Weight, or the lack of it, is a prime consideration, and when preparing for a ride can cause agonies. One problem is the unpredictable British weather and the need to be prepared for the worst. Fortunately, much current equipment is lightweight and the central piece of the cycle camper's armoury – the tent – is usually less than 8 lb (3.6 kg) in all, the groundsheet, flysheet and flexipoles included. Indeed, the new 'Jetpacker' weighs only 3 lb (1.4 kg). Other items such as sleeping bag and stove will be more bulky than heavy and this is a problem in itself.

Sort out essentials, err on the side of discretion and be ruthless in eliminating fripperies.

Store the last things you need at the bottom of the panniers. Store waterproofs near the top, and have snacks, drinks and first-aid kit easily accessible. And the tool kit.

There can be no substitute for experience, and the beginner should seek the advice of experts when choosing. The equipment may be expensive, but never as costly as a mistake. Here are some sources of information:

1. The Association of Cycle and Lightweight Campers (qv). Its membership has a wealth of experience made available through its Bulletins, etc.
2. Commercial firms include:
   (a) Backpacker Systems, 44 Winchcombe Street, Cheltenham ☎ Cheltenham 42200. Cycle camping specialists; send for price lists.
   (b) Field & Trek (Equipment) Ltd, 23–5 King's Road, Brentwood, Essex ☎ 0277 221259/ 219418/210913. Send for catalogue (80pp, 2,000 items) and Gear Guide (full of facts, figures and advice on outdoor gear).
3. For campsites, the best list available is that of the AC & LC (see Chapter 1). See also, the CTC handbook.
4. Articles on cycle camping appear from time to time in the cycling press.
5. See Books, Chapter 11.
6. The Fell Club welcomes contact with cycle

campers. As well as issuing a simple magazine, it has access to special camping sites.

Honorary Secretary: Cynthia Bladon, Kerk Nurseries, Coal Aston, Sheffield S18 6BE.

Cycle Hire

Hiring cycles is a particularly useful way for families to be awheel on holiday, away from the problems of motor traffic.

Many people live near to beauty spots where cycling would be ideal. It usually happens though that they also live in urban areas of dense and busy traffic, and the roads to the cycling area are far too dangerous to ride without anxiety in the company of small children. Where cycle hire exists in rural areas or places of scenic beauty, the family, or other groups, can travel there by any means available and then cycle in the freedom of the area reached.

Opportunities for cycle hire have increased rapidly in recent years. Most seaside resorts, national parks, country parks, market towns, etc., now have cycle hire facilities. In some places, notably in sparsely populated rural areas, cycle hire is a risky business. Hire companies may not open following their first bad season. It is wise to check by telephone or letter before planning an excursion in such areas. The number of cycles, and accessories, also varies. Most cycle hire companies are well established though and their facilities continue to expand.

As illustrations of the type of hire available, descriptions are given here of the hire facilities in a national park, and of a small private company in a localised area.

The Peak District

The Peak District has several cycle hire centres within easy reach of Sheffield and the Manchester area.

1. *Derwent Cycle Hire* is based on the superb Ladybower reservoir. The hire centre is at Fairholme picnic site, 2 miles north of Ashopton Viaduct on the A57, halfway between Sheffield and Glossop. The 7-mile trail follows the eastern bank of the reservoir, crosses at Fairholme and hugs the western bank along Derwent Dale to the Yorkshire border near Slippery Stones ☎ Hope Valley 52161.

2–3. *Ashbourne Cycle Hire*, and *Parsley Hay Cycle Hire* are at opposite ends of the Tissington Trail which goes north from Ashbourne to meet the High Peak Trail at Parsley Hay station, just short of Buxton. Ashbourne Cycle Hire is at Mapleton Lane picnic site about a quarter of a mile from the Market Place ☎ Ashbourne 43156. Parsley Hay Cycle Hire is at the old railway station off the A515, 8 miles south of Buxton ☎ Hartington 493.

For details about these three centres contact: Peak Park Joint Planning Board, Aldern House, Baslow Road, Bakewell, Derbyshire DE4 1AE ☎ 062-981 4321.

4. *Middleton Top Cycle Hire* is at the southern end of the High Peak Trail (the old High Peak Mineral rail line) which meets the Tissington Trail at Parsley Hay. The Hire Centre is just south of Matlock and Cromford on the B5023 ☎ Wirksworth 3204.

For further details contact: County Planning Officer, County Offices, Matlock, Derbyshire DE4 3AG ☎ 0629 3411 Ext 7121.

(NB An excellent triangular circuit of 40 miles would be to use the Tissington and High Peak Trails combined with the B5035 Wirksworth–Ashbourne road.)

5. *Lynne Park Cycle Hire* is on the extreme western edge of the Peak, convenient for Stockport and Man-

chester, and is in a country park near Disley (A6, 7 miles south of Stockport). The neighbouring country-side combines the splendour of high Sponds Hill, and the low-lying rural lanes around Adlington.

6. *Monsal Head Cycle Hire* is situated behind Monsal Head Hotel, 4 miles north of Bakewell on the B6465. It is within easy reach of Chatsworth (6 miles), Millers Dale (4 miles) and the lovely well-dressing villages of Tideswell and Eyam.

The machines they have for hire include:
Small wheel unisex, 3-speed,
Ladies/Gents tourist, 3-speed,
Junior sports (18-inch frame) 5-speed,
Ladies/Gents lightweight sports (19½–24½ inch frames), 5-speed,
Children's single speed,
Tandem, small wheel, 3-speed, with kiddi-seat.
Contact: Monsal Head, Bakewell, Derbyshire ☎ Great Longstone 505, Tideswell 871679.

Rutland Water Cycling
Rutland Water is a huge reservoir in Leicestershire. Most of the many miles of waterside tracks have been made available to cyclists by the Anglian Water Authority. A cycle hire company operates at the Water; it has a full range of machines, including bicycles with stabilisers for children down to four years, and 5-speed adult tricycles with two kiddi-seats. The tracks around the Water are entirely traffic free except where they meet picnic sites. In addition, the countryside around is quietly rural with many picturesque limestone villages, plus the larger towns of Oakham and Stamford.
Contact: Rutland Water Cycling, Whitwell Car Park, Oakham Leicestershire LE15 8BL ☎ 078-086 705.
(NB Most hire firms will quote special rates or give discounts for families and larger groups. Deposits and

evidence of identity (driving licence, banker's card) will almost always be required.)

The Agency for Camping, Caravan and Cycle Holidays, Hiring Equipment (ACHE) has a register of firms throughout Britain which hire cycles and accessories. The register includes firms from places as far apart as the Isle of Mull and Bovey Tracey, and the Agency can be contacted to find out if there are cycle hire facilities in the area where you wish to holiday.

Contact: ACHE, 12 St David's Hill, Exeter, Devon EX4 3RQ.

Fixed-centre Holidays and Tours

Chief among these are tours led by enthusiasts in their favourite territory. *Cycletouring* magazine advertises several such weeks and tours. They are not organised by the CTC but are led by CTC members on a voluntary basis. The table overleaf gives a breakdown of a typical set of tours available within the calendar year. The venues vary from year to year but this gives some idea of the range and scope on offer.

All abilities and tastes are catered for, in a way that could hardly be bettered if it was deliberately planned. The tours extend from April to November, ranging throughout Britain and as far afield as Iceland and the Black Forest region of Germany. They vary from three to fifteen days, from leisurely pottering along English lanes to pass-storming in the Pyrenees.

Select your tour according to taste. Read the rubrics: 'leader riding tandem with five year old', and 'nine year old riding solo', are really saying: 'the newest, rawest, feeblest recruit to cycling need not fear the pace'. Or, conversely, 'if you want to bomb along at 25 mph using 100+ gears for six hours at a stretch, don't join *us*'.

Families on a limited budget would welcome staying at a 'minimum facility' farm only if they were assured that all the basic needs of small children or babies could be catered for adequately. The fact must be borne in mind that those who most need the cheapest holidays can least afford to be spartan. The breadth of choice is available but some shrewd reading between the lines must be done before decisions are made.

Always compare prices. For example, in 1983 an eight-day holiday in the Peak District cost £120, but a Majorca equivalent only £165 for twelve days – more than £1 a day cheaper.

Although the CTC does not organise the holidays, it would not advertise or be associated with them unless it was convinced of the quality of leadership.

Leader training courses are held as natural leaders often emerge from the ranks of tour groups and ask for guidance and expertise before taking parties themselves.

In December 1979, twenty-three people attended such a tour leaders' course held at Hartington Youth Hostel. Four experienced tour leaders and the chairman of the CTC's Touring Development Committee offered information in such vital areas as taking teenagers on holiday, organising holidays abroad, hostelling and fixed-centre tours in Britain, insurance cover and first aid. Of those who attended, eleven led or shared leadership of CTC tours the following year. Regular tour leaders' courses are now held.

Typical Cycling Weeks and Tours – (*Cycletouring* Magazine)

Place	Starts	Days	Quotes from tour descriptions
1 Rutland	April	5	50 mpd in undulating country, including golden ironstone villages and Rutland Water.
2 Somerset	April	6	Youth Hostels. Easy Pace. 11–15 year olds.
3 France	April	3	'Cider Tour' based on St Lo.
4 Petworth	May	8	West Sussex. Guest House. Pub lunches. 40 mpd.
5 Lake District & Yorkshire	May	9	Leisurely pace in hill country. Youth hostels.
6 Long Mynd & Shropshire	May	6	Private hotel. Mixed age group. Walking and leisurely riding.
7 Holland	May	15	
8 Wiltshire	May	3	Mini break for younger age group. Salisbury Y H.

Place	Starts	Days	Quotes from tour descriptions
9 Northern Brittany	May	9	35 mpd. Mixed group but families welcome. Leader riding tandem with 5 year old.
10 Yorkshire	May	8	Superior YHs. James Herriot's Yorkshire. 50 mpd in hilly terrain.
11 Perthshire	June	6	50–60 mpd at 10 mph. Visits to castles etc.
12 Portugal	June	15	Tour of mountains. Inexpensive cuisine and wine. Flying London Heathrow.
13 N. Switzerland Austria Bavaria	June	15	Mixed age group. Leisurely/moderate pace. Air from Birmingham or Manchester to Zurich.
14 Isle of Man	June	8	Fixed centre using guest houses. Cliff and mountain scenery. Leisurely pace.

Place	Starts	Days	Quotes from tour descriptions
15 Iceland	June	15	Camping/hostel tour for experienced and self-reliant tourist. Unmetalled roads.
16 S. Ireland	June	15	All ages welcome. 30–60 mpd – 3 nights at each hostel. Group travel Holyhead–Galway.
17 Snowdonia	June	9	Strenuous. Rugged mountains. Hostels.
18 Hereford-shire	June	7	Fixed centre friendly hotel. Low mileage. Younger newcomers welcome but must be 18+.
19 Norwegian Fjords	June	16	Strenuous. Mountains. Fly London–Bergen.
20 Black Forest	June	13	Moderate pace. Fly Heathrow–Stuttgart.
21 Holland	July	7	Join in LAURA[1] rides of Dutch Touring Club.

Place	Starts	Days	Quotes from tour descriptions
22 Peak District	July	7	Peak Park Study Centre. Lectures.
23 Holland	July	10	AIT Rally[2] based near Arnhem. Choice of rides.
24 New Forest	July	6	7th Annual New Forest Cycling Week.[3] All ages.
25 S. W. Eire	July	14	Join one or both weeks. Exploring rides.
26 Black Forest	July	11	Train assisted YH tour. Primarily 11–15 years.
27 Spain	August	15	Strenuous. Must like mountain climbing and Spanish food. Basque & Picos de Europe.
28 Somerset	August	8	Superb country hotel in Quantocks.
29 Denmark	August	17	45 mpd. Boat from Harwich–Esbjerg.

	Place	Starts	Days	Quotes from tour descriptions
30	East Anglia	August	8	YH tour. 11–15 years, suitable for beginners.
31	Shropshire & Welsh Border	August	9	
32	Anglesey	August	8	Family riders and potterers. Informal. Farm site – 'minimum facility'.
33	Mid-Wales	August	7	Farm base. Home produced food. Tough country.
34	Shropshire	September	8	50 mpd based on Cleeve Hill YH.
35	France	September	9	Massif Central. Hilly terrain. Air to Clermont.
36	Scotland	September	7	Wild Highlands from Pitlochry. Rough stuff.
37	Devon	October	8	Fixed centre. All ages.

Place	Starts	Days	Quotes from tour descriptions
38 Somerset/ Dorset	October	8	Cheddar–Mendips– Quantocks– Blackdown Hills.
39 Minorca	November	8	Exploring. Fly E. Midlands Airport with cycles.

[1] LAURA rides – a four-day circuit based on the Amsterdam–Utrecht–Rotterdam triangle, organised by the Dutch Touring Club. Rides about 40 miles per day.

[2] AIT Rally – Alliance Internationale de Tourisme. The annual rally of the world cycle tourist organisation, held in a different country each year. A party always goes from Britain – however far afield.

[3] New Forest Cycling Week – cycling and camping weeks held with the cooperation of the Forestry Commission. Hundreds of cyclists are attracted to the Roundhill, Brockenhurst campsite (some staying in local bed-and-breakfasts). Many organised rides in the Forest plus longer runs as far as the Isle of Wight.

Commercial Holidays

Holidays for cyclists offered by commercial operators are growing in number.

A study of the advertisements for these holidays shows that the cyclist is very prominent in the planning (not a factor that one could necessarily assume, especially if the holiday was planned by non-cyclists). The cyclists' desire for freedom is acknowledged, itineraries and route-sheets are usually provided, secure facilities for cycles are often specified and much thought seems to be given to the variety of cycling knowledge and skills which must be allowed for.

As an example of holidays provided by para-cycling organisations, the YHA 'Ready Routes' scheme may be cited. Instead of the cyclist working out a route and writing to several hostels, he can follow a specially prepared route which needs a single booking. A week's accommodation including food is very reasonably priced. The routes between hostels are described and include information on nearby places of interest. Circular routes available for cyclists are limited (as yet) to the Lake District, Snowdonia and East Anglia, but more are planned.

The YHA also provides three other kinds of tours, each lasting a week. There are tours during July and August for young people (bikes not supplied) in North Yorkshire, moors and coast; South Downs and coast; West of the Wye; Suffolk and Essex; and Wild (!) Wales (see article 'So You Think They're not "proper" Cyclists?', *Cycling* (16 August 1980), YHA adventure holiday based at Bala, North Wales).

Secondly, between April and September there are family tours, with bikes supplied, in Essex, Suffolk and the North Norfolk coast.

Thirdly, there are individual tours, with cycle supplied, between April and September, in Norfolk, Suffolk, Yorkshire and Scotland.

The Scottish YHA offers organised tours – cycles provided by Highland Cycle Tours – with experienced leaders. For example, there were three 1982 one-week tours from Kingussie, visiting Strathspey, Braemore, Pitlochry and Glen Garry.

Contact: SYHA, 7 Glebe Crescent, Stirling FK8 2JA ☎ 0786 2821.

Commercial holidays based on a hotel or centre fall between two extremes: the hotel which reserves a week or two of the year specifically for cyclists, and the firm which provides full-season or all-the-year-round facilities. A more comprehensive list of addresses, with a précis of provision, is given below, but a few examples are given in more detail first.

The advertisement reads: 'Cycle touring in Mid-Wales. 8–15 September. For a week in autumn we invite you to experience cycletouring in superb un-spoilt countryside, using our restored seventeenth century farmhouse as your base (2 miles from BR station). All meals and suggested itineraries are pro-vided and a relaxed atmosphere is assured. Cyclists are welcome throughout the year for short or long stays. Contact: Mrs Susan Youell, Castell-y-dail, Mochdre Road, Newton, Powys.'

How could one resist so warm-hearted a welcome? Cyclists could answer such an advertisement with full confidence and anticipate a marvellous holiday.

In some cases cycletouring experts use the commer-cial centre as a base for specially-led tours. Coombe Cross Hotel, Bovey Tracey, Devon, and Otterburn Hall, Northumberland, are two hotels offering fully organised cycling weeks. The latter is in the beautiful border country near to Northumberland National Park and Kielder Forest. It is set in 85 acres of grounds and offers tennis, squash, croquet and even dancing for those who have not quite pedalled every last bit of energy out of their legs in the day's cycling!

A leaflet issued by the Field Studies Council lured a *Cycletouring* article writer from his home in the Northumberland border country to the Welsh border-land near Shrewsbury. He signed up for a week's course which included leisurely cycling in the com-pany of experts to help interpret the geology, land-forms, and local and natural history of the countryside being cycled through. His article ('ate lunch in a bus shelter during a heavy shower of snow . . . tea in a CTC recommended shop . . . tea on the banks of a mere watching herons . . . our focal point around four, each afternoon, was a tea shop') describes

fascinating rides to the Long Mynd, the Breiddons, Ironbridge, and the Shropshire Union Canal. The Field Studies Council has nine residential centres offering short (weekend or week-long) courses where, under expert guidance, the cyclist can learn more about the countryside.
Contact: Field Studies Council, Preston Montford, Montford Bridge, Shrewsbury SY4 1HW.

Additional Holidays

Freewheeling Holidays provide Wessex and Cotswolds tours, accommodation in hotel or guest house bed-and-breakfast, with cycles and full itineraries.
9 Kandahar, Aldbourne, Marlborough, Wiltshire ☎ Marlborough 40069.

Freewheeling Yorkshire organise both long tours in Yorkshire and guided day trips in York itself. Accommodation is in guest houses, and cycle hire is available.
16 Lawrence Street, York YO1 3BN ☎ 0904 20606.

John's Bike Tours One- or two-week tours from Bath. Luggage carried; breakfast cooked; mechanic and service car.
London Road, Bath, Avon ☎ 0225 310859.

Just Pedalling Seven-day itineraries in East Anglia with cycle hire if desired. Accommodation in hostels and guest houses.
43 Bracondale, Norwich NR1 2AT ☎ 0603 24071.

Otterburn Hall Hotel provides a week's holiday with half or full day tours. Half board and accommodation at the hotel.
Otterburn, Northumberland NE19 1HE ☎ 0830 20663.

Peak Park Study Centre organises several cycling weeks, one for beginners, in the Peak National Park. Full board, and evening activities as desired.
Losehill Hall, Castleton, Derbyshire S30 2WB ☎ 0433 20373.

Two Wheeler Tours Tours of about 30 miles a day in Devon and Dorset. Routes and campsites arranged. Luggage carried in mechanics' van.
8 Overbury Road, Parkstone, Poole, Dorset BH14 9JL ☎ 0202 741962.

Best Western Hotels offer two-day easy cycling holidays at 3-star hotels in the Cotswolds, cycles and itinerary provided.
Interchange House, 26 Kew Road, Richmond, Surrey TW9 2NA ☎ 01-940 9766.

Bike Events organise day excursions and holidays up to two weeks in length, all found.
66 Walcot Street, Bath, Avon ☎ 0225 65786.

Carefree Costwold Holidays offer all-year-round one-week unguided tours of the Cotswolds. Accommodation is in guest houses, farms and inns. Luggage is carried and cycle hire is available.
3 Cudnall Street, Charlton Kings, Cheltenham, Gloucestershire GL53 8HS ☎ 0242 28378.

Countryman Leisure Ltd Holidays in East Anglia of up to seven nights by flexible arrangement. Cycles provided. Accommodation in farms and inns.
49 High Street, Leiston, Suffolk ☎ 0728 830250.

East Anglian Cycling Holidays organise holidays in most of Britain's finest touring areas. Accommodation in guest and farmhouses. Cycle hire available.
The Bookshop, Yoxford, Suffolk 1P17 3BR ☎ 072-877 246.

Freedom of Ryedale Holidays offer weekend or weekly tours, guided or otherwise, in North Yorkshire. Accommodation in hostels, hotels or guest houses. Cycles provided, and full itineraries.
23a Market Place, Helmsley, North Yorkshire YO6 5BJ ☎ 0439 70775.

Push & Pedal All-inclusive one-week tours from Woodbury, near Exeter. Bed-and-breakfast and evening meal accommodation in inns or farmhouses. Cycles and all facilities provided. Radio breakdown service.
Swinfen, Knowle, Budleigh Salterton, Devon ☎ 03954 3738.

Bike Britain specialises in school party holidays. Accommodation is in hotels with breakfast, packed lunch and evening meal. All facilities, including bicycles, are provided, with a twelve-hour cycle repair or replacement service.
Cedar Cottage, Bristol Road, Thornbury, Bristol ☎ Thornbury 0454 413131.

10

HEALTH AND HANDICAP

Generations of fit and healthy cyclists have paid tribute to the bicycle as a means of getting and staying fit and healthy.

I met an elderly person in the street one day whom I had known for several years. She was getting on a Moulton cycle, pretty shakily. I knew that she had been unwell for some time. I had never seen her on a bike before and asked her how long she had been riding. A couple of weeks, she told me, then went on quite vehemently: 'I've had chronic back trouble. They've been taking me 20 miles by ambulance to hospital just to sit me on an exercise bike. So I've cancelled the therapy and bought a bike. It's grand.'

The vast majority of cyclists, however, are fit and healthy *because* they cycle. They did not take up cycling to get fit; they cycle because they enjoy it, and the fitness they achieve is just one of several by-products.

It is not far from the truth, though, to say that cycling can become an obsession – and some words of caution are necessary.

Many a cyclist, having planned a ride, will cycle in spite of being unwell and thus make himself worse. Many cyclists, too, will cycle through illnesses in a dour, determined, kill-or-cure fashion. It is really up to each cyclist, based on his own experience, to decide whether to keep cycling when unwell, or to rest. With such illnesses as sore throats and severe chest colds it is wise to keep warm and rest. With more serious illnesses such as 'flu there will be little choice, and only a fool would even contemplate a ride under such conditions.

Most cyclists are basically fit and can be on the bike almost every day of the year. And this can bring its danger. It will be impossible to sustain peak fitness week in, week out. As the days shorten, especially where long and hard cycle rides are fitted in at the end of a busy day, the cyclist will be living near to the limit of his resources. Then a sweaty tiring ride in freezing fog or in the bitterly cold night air will leave him prone to attack at the point of his weakness: a sore throat, lumbago, even bronchitis may result.

A danger in being super-fit and being (even modestly) proud of it, and of feeling fit, is that we can believe ourselves to be indestructible, quite incapable of the weaknesses and maladies of feeble, spindly-legged, sedentary mortals. We should not be so fooled. The harder a cyclist rides or trains the more he should be aware of the need to balance work output with good food intake, physical demands with sensible physical preparation and precaution, regular exercise with proper rest and relaxation.

The cyclist should also be sensible to the essential requirements of diet, clothing, cycle design, cycle adjustment, etc., faults in which can lead to short-term discomfort or long-term chronic disorder. No cyclist should leave himself open to failure where forethought and sensible planning can guarantee success.

A novice cyclist should not ride too far with the wind behind him; the time will come when he needs to turn for home and he may find himself short of the physical strength needed to make it in comfort. Most cyclists know about 'the bonk'. It is a physical condition of utter weakness, sometimes accompanied by dizziness, faintness and cold sweats, brought on by cycling too far or too fast without sufficient rest and food intake. Under 'bonk' conditions a faint breeze seems like a strength-sapping wind; a level road, an unrideable hill; the bottom bracket seems to have locked and the pedals refuse to turn.

The fault is not in the machine, but in the body. A person with 'the bonk' will recover quickly if he can rest awhile, drink some hot sweet tea and eat some chocolate or other energy-giving food. If he finds himself stranded some miles from home with no such resources he is unlikely to get 'the bonk' ever again: he will either be far better prepared on all subsequent excursions, or never go back to recover the bike he threw in the ditch!

Even experienced cyclists can be led into indiscretions. I knew a cyclist who made a New Year resolution to go out on his bike every day of the year, even if it was only for a mile. It sounds a laudable idea. He got to October without missing a day, but by that time his resolution had become dogged stupidity. He should probably have stayed in and read a cycling magazine the day he went out, caught some virus the doctors never identified, and slipped into a dissipated state that only several weeks of careful nursing brought him out of.

Health is a gift. It is precious; far too precious to put in jeopardy by neglect or folly. It is for this reason that I applaud the aim of the British Cycling Coaching Scheme (BCCS) – see Chapter 1 – to put a trained coach into every cycling club. Many cyclists, of course, do not belong to clubs. Even those who do, may only be members to enjoy the social life or other benefits and have no pretensions towards becoming a super athlete. Fine. The best part about cycling is being out on the bike. I do not subscribe to the view that a cyclist is any less a cyclist because he does not race, do circuit training, bodybuilding, etc. Even so,

the most casual, unadventurous cyclist will do well to
heed the accumulated advice and wisdom of the many
experienced cyclists who pass on their expertise. Failure to do so could lead to short-term or permanent
incapacity which ought otherwise to be avoided.

For example, knee trouble (tendinitis) finished
Bernard Hinault's 1980 Tour de France, and Cyrille
Guimard's racing career. This injury, caused by over-
use of the tendon, could happen even to the potter-
type rider since it is caused also by strain, especially in
cold or wet weather, using gears which are too big,
bad riding position, wrong saddle height, a twisted
pedal, etc. The cure could be slow, including rest,
heat treatment and embrocations, and prevention is
far better. It is for this reason – educating people
about the health aspects of cycling – that I urge cyclists
to join a local club; then, if they develop saddle sores,
or knee pains, or back trouble, they can talk the
problem through with other cyclists who will be able
to give them simple tips or remedies, but mostly,
encouragement, since many maladies are common
and need not last long or prevent full enjoyment of
being awheel.

Another way of learning about the whole business
of sensible cycling is through the cycling press. Most
of the cycling papers feature regular articles, either by
successful cyclists, by coaches of high reputation, or
by doctors, on the broad subject of exercise and
health. Most publications also encourage correspond-
ence about health problems and get an expert to give
specific advice.

Many cycling books, too, include chapters on
health. See, for example, a chapter by Dr Christopher
Woodard in *The Raleigh Book of Cycling* (ed. R.
Shaw) which explores common fallacies, cycling ail-
ments (see how many you've got, or have had!),
eating habits, women cyclists (allays fears about pro-

ducing 'big, unfeminine muscles') and bravely specifies the ideal cyclist. I've just read it again and thought it was me, until I got to the bit about 'being ruthless in training . . .'!

The cyclist should remember that everybody is unique. A dozen experts may give a dozen different diagnoses of an ailment, and suggest a dozen different remedies or prognoses, but in the end it all becomes a matter of opinion and the cyclist himself will have to take that advice which seems to be the most appropriate to his particular case. If you are sensible, eat well, cycle regularly but not always fast or too far, and keep warm, you may be reassured on two points: however baffling or contradictory the experts' advice seems, if you just keep cycling you will keep fit, and, should you fall ill and the experts give a gloomy forecast, the testimony of many in similar circumstances is that they proved the experts wrong, by sheer guts.

The latter part of this chapter is a tribute to such cyclists. Hopefully, too, it will encourage many whose incapacities might otherwise stop them from getting awheel.

The medical profession recognises the value of cycling as a health-maintaining pastime and as a vital ingredient in the treatment of many illnesses and afflictions.

The Association of British Cycling Doctors (ABCD) is at the forefront in monitoring both the beneficial effects of cycling and the problems which arise from excessive or strenuous exercise. Thus, at a recent annual meeting held at Chase Farm Hospital Postgraduate Centre, Enfield, they considered papers on exercise-induced asthma, cardiac problems in sport, and muscle fatigue. The three-day meeting included – what else? – a 10-mile time trial and a cycle tour.

Many handicapped people reveal both ingenuity and determination in rising above their disability. Despite having only one leg, or perhaps because of it, twenty-four year old Paul Coleman rode 80 miles in two days from Eastleigh, Hampshire, to London, to raise money for the disabled. This generous, unself-pitying attitude pervades the cycling fraternity, and handicapped cyclists in particular.

I met John Barritt, a cyclist from Binham in Norfolk, pedalling easily in the narrow lanes near his home. Only later did I learn that a serious back injury had resulted in the shortening of one of his legs. He simply made one of his cycle cranks longer!

I own a tricycle which once belonged to a teenager who had polio. He used the machine to get himself back to mobility, and having done so emigrated to South Africa. Robert Williams was confined to a wheelchair with multiple sclerosis, but he also got himself a tricycle and used his engineering abilities to adapt the pedals so that they swung upright to keep his feet in position. He now cycles considerable distances and with genuine altruism raises money for research into the illness he refuses to give in to.

There is no doubt that cycling speeds recovery from illness or operation. The exercise strengthens muscles and especially that superb muscle, the heart, and gets the healing blood pounding through the body. South Londoner Keith Gibson had a kidney transplant at St Heliers hospital, his mother donating the kidney. A mere three weeks later he was cycling again. Keith Castle, the now famous heart transplant personality, has done much for cycling and the recognition of its therapeutic value by constantly riding his bike and unashamedly publicising the fact. He was 'advised by doctors to take up regular cycling to regain fitness after the operation and to help maintain it'. Recognising his contribution to cycling, the British Cycling

Bureau honoured him with their Gold Award for Cycling.

Ken Davies, at fifty-one years old the most venerable of heart transplant patients, regained fitness by using an exercise bicycle in hospital and was advised to cycle 6 miles every day. How many fit cyclists manage that? It totals a steady 2,170 miles a year. Peter Walthall had major heart surgery but was soon back on his machine – one month later – and quickly began riding for two hours at a stretch without difficulty.

Several top-class racing cyclists have suffered heart trouble, yet have been undaunted by it. In 1965 Dave Gabbott, having already established himself as a superb racing cyclist, suffered a disordered heart beat and periods of acute breathlessness. Hospital doctors advised him to tone his racing down. He did so briefly and then, over a deliberate twelve-year period, gradually built up his strength and became the first person to break through the two-hour barrier for a 50-mile ride by tricycle.

Both Geoff Salter – who has a heart block – and Dave Lloyd, with a condition called extra systole, are international road racing cyclists. Their hearts have been monitored on hospital treadmills and they both produced records on an exercise test. Both men are top-flight speed merchants and Dave has many distance records to his credit, including the End to End.

The name Reg Harris was a household name after the Second World War. Some years after giving up cycling he suffered a minor heart attack and this acted as a warning to him. He made a remarkable return to sprint racing when well into his fifties and at the age of sixty he returned to competitive cycling as an amateur, riding in time trials 'to keep fit'. He admits that he has not found it easy to go out when the weather is bad, but the racing provides the necessary incentive. 'At the moment, if I miss a day or two I soon notice it; even a canal bridge feels like a hill.'

A severe handicap is blindness. As blind people approach middle age they begin to lose their sense of balance, a lack of self-confidence sets in and they withdraw more and more to the security of their homes. Cycling provides not only exercise to keep the body fit but also that essential balance, and the confidence derived from the exhilaration of being out in the streaming air. Here the tandem comes into its own, with a sighted 'steerer' and blind or partially sighted 'stoker'. I know from experience that the blind stokers are fearless as they trust themselves to their sighted pilots. In the Uppingham area of Rutland in Leicestershire we have a group of steerers who tandem with a solicitor, a chicken farmer, a secretary, etc. In addition we take out groups who are sometimes physically and mentally disabled as well as being blind and their rides with us are the first time ever on a machine. Their courage and good humour is an inspiration. Leicestershire cyclists wishing to help as steerers can contact the 'Rutland Blind Tandem Riders' via the Secretary, Royal Leicestershire, Rutland and Wycliffe Society for the Blind, Margaret Road, Evington, Leicester. Similar schemes operate nationwide.

Hammersmith Borough Council's tandem club includes four tandems, and their contact is: Beata Duncan-Jones, Social Services Area 1 Offices, 160 Coningham Road, London W12 ☎ 01-749 3331 Ext 57.

The Solihull Association for the Blind organises tandem riding. Their seven tandems are steered by a team of twenty-five to thirty riders with twenty stokers. They have taken part in such events as the Great Midland Bike Ride to Stratford, organised by the Birmingham Bicycling Campaign (Pushbikes). They are currently in need of a 20-inch frame machine for two smaller riders.* This blind association is being supported by Birmingham University's Athletic Union CC whose 'Tandem Fund' has the Lord Mayor of Birmingham as patron. Contact: Ian Bailey, at the University.

Both 'In-Tandem' (Contact: Inter-Action, 15 Wilkin Street, London NW5 3NX ☎ 01-267 9471 or FLAG, 10 Priory Street, York ☎ York 21133), and the Worcester College for the Blind ☎ 0905 354627 put teams in the End to End ride during the International Year for Disabled People. 'In-Tandem' provide both tandems and triplets, and their steerers, stokers and supporters attend the York Rally.

Metropolitan Police Cadets at Sunbury Training Centre, Middlesex, support the Avenue Centre, Normansfield Hospital, Teddington – a centre for mentally handicapped people who are often also blind. A senior instructor at the latter centre is a partially sighted keen cyclist. The centres held a joint End to End ride to raise funds for the hospital.

Anyone living in or near Newcastle who can help as a steerer should contact: Miss D. J. Robinson, Mobility Officer for the Blind, Civic Centre, Newcastle-on-Tyne ☎ Newcastle 28520 Ext: 5320.

A similar need exists in Coventry where a scheme to buy special tandems is organised. Contact: Kathie Bellingham, 2 Brisban Court, Croft Pool, Bedworth, Coventry.

The Merton Sports and Recreation Club for the Visually Handicapped has a tandem scheme as part of its policy of providing outdoor activities for blind and partially-sighted members. Steerers are always

* The Lady Zia Wernher School, Stopsley, Luton, needs 16-inch frame tricycles for its children who have impaired balance, but the machines are out of production. If you can help, contact Trevor Humphries – a Bedfordshire DA member – on 0582 21058.

needed. Contact: Mrs R. Crouch, 23 Broadlands Way, New Malden, Surrey ☎ 942 2053.

The Tandem Club (qv) is involved in providing steerers in such places as Glasgow, Kent, Nottingham and the West Midlands. Members of the club, or others interested in extending their activities, should contact Mrs Sue Atkins, 3 Kenmore Lodge, Mortlake Road, Kew, Surrey TW9 3JQ.

The CTC's Touring and Countryside Trust is helping to coordinate the support that is being given. It would welcome comments from existing steerers and stokers on their experience and difficulties, and be pleased to hear from tandem owners willing to act as steerers or able to loan or donate tandems to organisations involved in blind work. Contact: Deputy Clerk to the Trust, Kenneth Cox, 52 King William Street, London EC4R 9AA.

Event organisers often include the blind in their plans. During the Spalding Bulb Festival there is a 26-mile event for tandems which has involved blind teams from throughout Britain, and also America and the Continent. Individual clubs run schemes also. London St Christopher's CCC has a hand-built Jack Taylor tandem which they are using in conjunction with local social agencies. They plan to provide more tandems in the future.

National agencies, too, are becoming aware of and beginning to provide for the healthy use of the cycle by fit and handicapped alike. Stung into action by acquiring the reputation: 'sick man of Europe', the Scottish Health Education Group, in conjunction with the Chest, Heart and Stroke Association, brought international cycling back to the Scottish calendar. Its 'Health Race', a July event of some 500 miles for top racing cyclists, is watched by thousands of Scots and holiday visitors. Its accompanying Health Week involves the public in many types of fitness testing and displays, cycle events and tandem rides for the blind at Bellahouston Park. For details of future plans, contact: Event Director, Scottish Health Education Group, Woodburn House, Canaan Lane, Edinburgh EH10 4SG ☎ 031-477 8044.

Manchester and Salford Health Education Units recently organised a one-day event to publicise cycling as a healthy leisure pursuit, and also to highlight difficulties for urban cyclists. A series of lectures was arranged at the Royal Exchange Theatre in St Anne's Square, including three on aspects of cyclists' rights, one on leisure cycling in a national park, and one on health, fitness and diet. For future plans contact: Health Education Centre, 45 Hardman Street, Manchester M3 3HD ☎ 834 8980 Ext 9.

Unlike old soldiers, old cyclists do die, but are healthy to the last. A veteran time triallist died recently during a 25-mile race at the age of seventy-seven. He only started cycling when seventy-two years old, having previously been a top steeplechase jockey. In 1981, a seventy-four year old covered 206 miles in a national 12-hour competition, just one of many such notable achievements. This letter, published in *Cycling*, is the epitome of sparkling health and humour:

'My great uncle, a keen if erratic cyclist at 90, owed his survival in no small measure to the forbearance of other road users. On one occasion he was stopped by a policeman who asked politely why he had ignored a 'one-way' sign. Replied uncle, unabashed: 'That's for visitors, I'm a resident.'

One of the grand old men of cycling is Doctor Clark-Kennedy of Cambridge, an ardent walker who completed the 270-mile Pennine Way in fifteen days when he was seventy-eight, and 'bagged over forty Munros – isolated peaks over 1,300 feet – since I was eighty'. Since having a hip-joint replacement operation, he has found walking difficult, owing to poor balance and weak muscles, but rides a bicycle with ease. He cannot mount a large machine but uses a folding Peugeot, intending 'to encourage other ageing people like myself to strive to remain active and thereby keep young'.

Keeping young is ninety year old W. S. Gibson, a retired solicitor who keeps on cycling 'to keep the legs in trim'. Way back in 1928 he broke the Land's End to London tandem record, and is also a keen tricyclist. Asked why he kept two trikes in his office he replied: 'Because I can't get three in!'

Handicapped and housebound? Want to get fit before getting out? Static bicycles may be the answer. Puch supply, free, a 16-page colour folder describing their exercise machines. Contact Steyr-Daimler-Puch (GB) Ltd, 211 Lower Parliament Street, Nottingham NG1 1FZ ☎ 0602 56521.

Did you know?
Cycling for 8 miles at 12 mph is equivalent to:
10 minutes of wrestling,
30 minutes of football or squash,
50 minutes of tennis,
60 minutes of skating,
2½ miles of brisk walking,
24 holes of golf.
(But much more enjoyable.)
From: *On Your Bike*, chapter 'Cycling & Health', by Dr Ronald Williams.

11

BOOKS, GUIDES AND FILMS

Books

A wealth of published material is available in the bookshops for either the armchair reader or the serious participant needing practical advice for getting and staying on the pedals.

Limits of space demanded condensing whole books into single phrases, but I hope the essence of the book comes through.

I have avoided such words as 'lavishly' in an attempt to be objective. Just occasionally, though, I have not resisted the expression of excitement on reading a particularly fine book.

Prices have been omitted, these being rarely stable; the number of pages is a better long-term guide to the relative cost.

ADAMS, Harry   *Cycle & Cycling* (Basil Blackwell, 1965) 63pp.
An easy-reading text for small children, covering the basics for safe enjoyment of the bicycle.

ADSHEAD, Robin   *Bikepacking for Beginners* (Oxford Illustrated Press, 1978) 85pp.
An illustrated introduction to lightweight camping using a cycle. The chapter on loading the machine is of value to all cycle tourists.

ADSHEAD, Robin   *Cycletouring* (Spur, 1981) 64pp.
Choosing a cycle; loading it for touring; hazards, etc.

ALDERSON, Frederick *Bicycles* (A. & C. Black, 1974) 64pp.
Traces the history of the bicycle and its development; includes basic maintenance. Suitable as a background reader for beginners. Illustrated with photographs and line drawings.

ALDERSON, Frederick *The Cyclists' Companion* (Robert Hale, 1981) 192pp.
A book of basics, tracing the development of cycling from its origin. A big part of the book is devoted to graded cycle tours throughout England, varying in duration from five to seven days.

ALDERSON, Frederick *Bicycling: A History* (David & Charles, 1972) 214pp.
An unusual treatment of cycle history, full of anecdotes and literary quotations. The growth of cycle sport is traced, and the cycle's use for social, economic and military purposes.

ALDERSON, Frederick *England by Bicycle* (David & Charles, 1974) 207pp.
After a break of twenty years the author takes to the pedals again and goes on a 1,350-mile tour of England.

ALTH, Max *All About Bikes and Bicycling* (Bailey Bros & Swinfen, 1972) 176pp.
A detailed manual, particularly for the beginner, on cycle maintenance and repair.

ANTHONY, Michael *The Games Were Coming* (Andre Deutsch, 1963) 223pp.
A novel set in Trinidad describing the events surrounding the Southern Games, and the hero's obsessive desire to be champion.

BALLANTINE, Richard *The Piccolo Bicycle Book* (Pan Books, 1977) 190pp.

A wide-ranging book of basics for young cyclists, it has a large and useful section devoted to maintenance and repair.

BALLANTINE, Richard   *Richard's Bicycle Book* (Pan Books, 1979) 383pp.
A comprehensive review of the cycle and its possibilities. Hours of fascinating reading, plenty of line illustrations and advice. Read the page about dogs (page 148).

BALLANTINE, Richard   *Basic Bicycle Repair* (paperback) (Rodale).

BANNISTER, Ted   *Better Roadcraft* (Kaye & Ward, 1973) 95pp.
A book for children on all aspects of cycling safety. It includes technical details of the cycle, RoSPA training with photographs and drawings, and some fascinating quizzes.

BENNETT, Hal Zina   *Complete Bicycle Commuter* (Sierra Club Books, 1982) 181pp.
Includes cycle secrets and safety tips.

BOWDEN, Gregory Houston   *The Story of the Raleigh Cycle* (W. H. Allen, 1975) 216pp.
A history of the cycle firm by the great-grandson of the founder. It includes anecdotes of great sportsmen associated with Raleigh, including Reg Harris and Peter Duker.

BRIDGE, Raymond   *Bicycle Touring* (Sierra Club Books, 1979) 456pp.
Everything from camping on tour to building a wheel.

BUDRYS, Ajay   *Bicycles – How They Work & How to Fix Them* (Rand McNally, 1976) 98pp.
A complete manual for the workshop enthusiast. Fully illustrated with 'exploded' diagrams and close-

up photographs which make following the text easy.

COLLIGAN, Doug *Cyclists' Manual* (Blandford, 1981) 160pp.
More than a manual; includes fitness, riding techniques and touring.

CROWLEY, Terence *Discovering Old Bicycles* (Shire Publications, 1973) 56pp.
A handy pocket book describing the history of cycles 1850–1950. Includes photographs.

DUKER, Peter *Sting in the Tail – By Racing Bicycle Around the World* (Pelham, 1973) 174pp.
An epic journey circling the globe in 7 months 16 days, and setting cycling records en route. Attacked by thugs in the Khyber Pass: '. . . blood was now pouring out of a gash in my scalp . . . turning my left shoulder a deep crimson'.

DURRY, Jean *The Guinness Guide to Bicycling* (Guinness Superlatives, 1977) 220pp.
Translated from the French and edited by J. B. Wadley, this is a superb book, beautifully produced, describing all facets of the cycling world.

EBEL, Suzanne *Explore the Cotswolds by Bicycle* (Ward Lock, 1973) 159pp.
Cycling trips (sic) based on thirteen different centres. Outward and homeward routes are described with a gazetteer of villages passed through. Distances are 10–32 miles, weekend tours up to 57 miles.

EMERSON, P. J. (Baha) *Inflation – Try a Bicycle* (36 Ballysillan Road, Belfast, 14) 147pp.
Wittily written – cycling in seven African countries.

ENGLISH, Ronald *Cycling for You* (Lutterworth Press, 1964) 176pp.

An experienced cycle tourist introduces the adventure of cycling to young readers – touring, racing and technical hints.

ENNIS, Philip *Rutland Rides* (Spiegl Press, Stamford, Lincs) 5 volumes 1979–83.
Cycle rides in Rutland and parts of Cambridgeshire, Leicestershire, Lincolnshire and Northamptonshire.

EVANS, David *The Ingenious Mr Pedersen* (Redwood Burn Ltd, Trowbridge, 1981) 132pp.
A history of the Dursley-Pedersen bicycle and its inventor.

EVANS, Humphrey *Freewheeling* (Octopus Books, 1982) 80pp.
A full colour book which describes the fun of cycling for all the family.

GAMBLING, Mick *On Cycling* (Forest Publishing, Coventry, 1982) 99pp.
Distilled humour of the 'Cycling' contributor; illustrated by Johnny Helms.

GAUSDEN, Christa *The CTC Route Guide to Cycling in Britain & Ireland* (Oxford Illustrated Press, 1980) 431pp.
A network of 365 inter-linking routes using 'quiet roads, preferably lanes . . .'. Sketchmaps and a gazetteer included.

GAUSDEN, Christa *Weekend Cycling* (Hamlyn, 1982) 256pp.
Routes from Somerset to Inverness, plus maps and information.

GRAY, Dennis *On My Own Feet* (Max Parrish, 1964) 192pp.
An account of a person handicapped from birth, and his fight to overcome. Very amusing in parts.

HAMMOND, Reginald (ed.)   *Explore Britain by Bicycle* (Ward Lock, 1971) 160pp.
Suggested tours on a county basis. Routes, distances and items of interest along the way.

HARRIS, Reg   *Two Wheels to the Top* (W. H. Allen, 1976) 218pp.
An autobiography of the best-known British cyclist, including his minor heart attack and his return to racing in 1974.

HAWKINS, Karen and Gary   *Bicycle Touring in Europe* (Sidgwick & Jackson, 1974) 200pp.
A refreshingly different style, full of useful advice. Ends with nine favourite tours from 'A taste of two wines' (France) to 'Castles and Cuckoo Clocks' (Germany).

HELMS, Johnny   *Transport of Delight* (1980) 88pp and *Round the Bends* 96pp (66 Norlands Lane, Widnes, Lancashire, 1981).
The inimitable cartoonist of 'Honk' fame.

HENDERSON, Noel   *Continental Cycle Racing* (Pelham, 1970) 192pp.
Gives a fascinating insight into the racing scene, including ten Classics, the three major Tours, and the World Championships.

HOBAN, Barry   *Watching the Wheels go Round* (Stanley Paul, 1981) 258pp.
Autobiography of a great British racing cyclist.

HUGHES, Tim   *Adventure Cycling in Britain* (Blandford, 1978) 231pp.
An experienced cyclist gives practical advice on choosing, using and coping with a bicycle; and suggests tours through Britain. Some useful appendices.

HUGHES, Tim   *Wheels of Choice* (Cyclographic, PO Box 20, Great Missenden, Buckinghamshire, 1981) 96pp
A selection of photographs by a noted cycling photographer.

HUNTER, Edmund   *The Story of the Bicycle* (Ladybird, 1975) 51pp.
A basic book for children, in full colour; includes history, organisations and maintenance.

HURNE, Ralph   *The Yellow Jersey* (Weidenfeld & Nicolson, 1973) 254 pp.
An entertaining novel set around an Englishman's attempt at the Tour de France.

JEROME, Jerome K.   *Three Men on the Bummel* (Dent, 1900) 192pp.
The eternally amusing novel of a long-distance cycle ride, complete with turn-of-the-century ideas on 'the perfect saddle', 'bearings falling apart', etc. (A Bummel? See page 192.)

KEARLEY, Claude   *The Hamlyn Book of Cycling* (Hamlyn, 1978) 61pp.
Large format, all colour book of basics for children. An exciting introduction to cycling as sport and pastime.

KNOTTLEY, Peter   *Cycle Touring in Europe* (Constable, 1975) 252pp.
A veteran cycle tourist yields his experience. Includes tips about the cycle, maps, camping, etc., information about Europe, how to get there and where to stay.

KONOPKA, Peter   *The Complete Cycle Sport Guide* (E P Publishing, 1981) 182pp.
The author is both racing cyclist and medical officer to the West German Cycling Federation.

MAGOWAN, Robin   *Tour de France* (Stanley Paul, 1979) 203pp.
A detailed account of the 75th anniversary race, including the drama of drugs and the first ever riders' strike.

MESSENGER, Chas   *Conquer the World* (Pelham, 1968) 148pp.
Contains all aspects of training and technique for road racing.

MESSENGER, Chas   *Cycling Crazy* (Pelham, 1970) 173pp
Descriptions of racing events the author witnessed as manager of the British team.

MESSENGER, Chas   *Cycling's 'Circus'* (Pelham, 1971) 183pp.
Graphic accounts of the Tour of Britain (now the Milk Race) from the 'hard luck' Tour of 1951 to the 1956 race when all the riders went off course.

MESSENGER, Chas   *Where There's a Wheel* (Pelham, 1972) 214pp.
After a brief, poignant lament for the demise of the BLRC the author describes the Tours of Britain 1958–64, which he organised.

MOORE, George   *The George Moore Collection* (Vols I–III) (Beekay Products, 23 Greenwich High Road, London SE10 8LU, 1980–2).
Books of the Victorian cycling cartoonist.

MURPHY, Dervla   *Full Tilt* (Murray, 1975) 271pp.
An Irish woman's ride from home to Afghanistan.

NELMS, Peter   *Cycle Sense* (TI Raleigh/RoSPA).
Colour picture-strip booklet aimed at making cycling safer, by the Nottinghamshire CC Road Safety Officer.

NICHOLSON, Geoffrey *The Great Bike Race* (Hodder & Stoughton, 1977) 192pp.
Based on the 1976 Tour, this is an appraisal of the French obsession with the greatest bike race in the world.

OSMAN, Tony *The New Cyclist* (Collins, 1982) 95pp.
Gives details of bicycle types, maintenance, pleasure cycling and distance riding.

PATTERSON, Frank *The Art of Frank Patterson* (Jim Willis, Hollyfast Road, Coventry, 1980–2).
Three volumes of the drawings of the renowned cycling artist.

PORTER, Hugh *Champion on Two Wheels* (Robert Hale, 1975) 187pp.
Autobiography of the four-times world pursuit champion.

RAKOWSKI, John *Adventure Cycling in Europe* (Rodale, 1981) 350pp.
Preparing for the tour; twenty-seven countries from Austria to Yugoslavia.

RAY, Alan J. *Cycling – Land's End to John o'Groats* (Pelham, 1971) 150pp.
Details the formation of the RRA and WRRA, and describes record-breaking End to End rides from the Victorian era to Dick Poole's 1965 record.

RITCHIE, Andrew *King of the Road* (Wildwood House, 1975) 192pp.
Large format, illustrated history of cycling. Scores of contemporary prints and photographs giving hours of enjoyable reading.

ROBERTS, Derek *The Invention of Bicycles & Motorcycles* (Usborne, 1975) 48pp.
Fully illustrated colour book for children, including some unusual comic cartoons.

ROBERTS, Peter   *Better Cycling* (Kaye & Ward, 1969) 79pp.
An illustrated beginners' book concentrating on safety and the RoSPA proficiency test.

ST PIERRE, Roger   *The Book of the Bicycle* (Ward Lock, 1973) 110pp.
Illustrates graphically all the healthy exuberance of being awheel, from cycling proficiency to massed-start racing.

SANDERS, William   *Backcountry   Bikepacking* (Rodale, 1982) 292pp.
Cycle camping – includes how to cope with wetness, hotness, blackness, scary stuff (traffic) and hostiles (yobboes).

SAUNDERS, David   *Cycling in the Sixties* (Pelham, 1971) 148pp.
Great stories of great cyclists from Addy to Zoetemelk, and of great events in cycle racing, by a leading cycling journalist.

SHAW, Reginald (ed.)   *The Raleigh Book of Cycling* (Peter Davies, 1975) 218pp.
Everything cycling, from proficiency to track racing; contributing authorities include J. B. Wadley, Les Warner, Tim Hughes, Ted Bannister and Rex Coley.

STREET, Roger T. C.   *Victorian High Wheelers* (Dorset Publishing, Sherborne, 1980) 60pp.
Mainly the rise and fall of Christchurch Bicycle Club (1876–90).

SUDBURY, Ronald F.   *The Bicycle & the Postage Stamp* (Harry Hayes, 1976) 62pp.
Hundreds of stamps illustrated, from the first ever of cycling (Germany 1887) to 1975, the earliest British being 1970!

SUMNER, Philip   *Early Bicycles* (Hugh Evelyn, 1966) 12pp, 12 plates.
An enthusiast's large format book of bikes between the hobby horse (1791) and the 'Golden' Sunbeam (1907).

THOMAS, Nigel   *City Rider* (Elm Tree Books, 1981) 126pp.
'How to survive with your bike.' The topics range from accidents and disasters to weather. Superb b/w photographs, and cartoons by Maddocks.

VERNON, Tom   *Fat Man on a Bicycle* (Michael Joseph, 1981) 288pp.
A humorous account of 19-stone Vernon's ca. 1,000-mile ride across France. His book begins: 'I began . . .' and ends (quite properly): '. . . on a bicycle.'.

WATSON, Richard, and Gray Martin   *Book of the Bicycle* (Penguin, 1978) 333pp.
History, cycle sport and maintenance. The 'stuckness' of a cotter pin lasts 2½ pages; a click when pedalling could be . . . your left knee.

WAY, R. John   *The Bicycle – A Guide and Manual* (Hamlyn, 1973) 96pp.
Covers all aspects of recreational cycling; by the former editor of *Cycletouring* magazine. Large format.

WILKINSON-LATHAM, Robert   *Cycles in Colour* (Blandford, 1978) 195pp.
Half a prose history of cycles, half colour plates and descriptions of cycles from 1818 to 1977.

WOODEFORDE, John   *The Story of the Bicycle* (Routledge & Kegan Paul, 1970) 175pp.
Well-researched history of the bicycle 1870–1969. Photographs, cartoons and contemporary sketches. Early gloomy forecasts of the deleterious effect of

cycling on the body are shown in a mock skeleton (page 141).

WOODLAND, Les   *Cycle Racing – Training to Win* (Pelham, 1975) 144pp.
A thorough manual for the enthusiast dealing with such topics as: fitness, road and gym training, diet and nutrition. Contains Fausto Coppi's eight commandments.

WOODLAND, Les *Cycle Racing and Touring* (Pelham, 1976) 133pp.
An introduction to the whole gamut of cycling – plenty of enthusiasm and authority. Juicy little glossary of cycling 'jargon'.

(Books may be ordered by post from: Selpress Books Ltd, 35 High Street, Wendover, Buckinghamshire HP22 6DU.)

Guides

In addition to suggested routes contained in cycling books, there are a growing number of slimmer publications available to help the planning of localised rides.
Cycling World has now produced six such guides to:
　Wales
　North West England
　East Anglia
　The Midlands
　Northern Highlands
　West Country
Contact: Stone Industrial Publications, Andrew House, 2a Granville Road, Sidcup, Kent DA14 4BN.
Cycling in Birmingham contains 20pp of maps of backstreet routes, information on the law, accidents,

bikes on trains, negotiation of roads to the city centre avoiding busy ring road and complex roundabouts. Designed to help new cyclists. Contact: Pushbikes, 54 Allison Street, Digbeth, Birmingham 5.

Edinburgh for Cyclists is a wide-ranging guide to city cycling routes, facilities, etc. Contact: Spokes, 2 Ainslie Place, Edinburgh EH3 6AR.

On Your Bike is a guide to cycling in London. It gives many useful addresses, advice on town riding, and a number of clear maps which show recommended routes avoiding main roads. Contact: Kensington & Chelsea Friends of the Earth, 93 Lexham Gardens, London W8.

Bike It A guide to cycling in North and East London (2nd, enlarged, edition). Published by Redbridge FoE, it lists shops, clubs, services and other facilities. Contact: Andy Marshall, 20 Talbot Gardens, Seven Kings, Ilford, Essex; or, The London Cycling Campaign, Colombo Centre, Colombo Street, London SE1; or FoE, Poland Street, London W1.

Cyclists' Guide to North Wales 80pp Written by John Holman, warden of Rhiwaedog Youth Hostel, Rhos-y-Gwaliau, Bala, Gwynedd LL23 7EU, it gives details of three week-long tours.

Guide to Cycling in and around London Bartholomew/CTC, from bookshops.

Guide to Nottingham is published by the Nottingham cyclists action group, Pedal Pushers. It is designed to help emerging cyclists, and in addition to maps and routes – both inner city and out into the country – it contains advice and tips on many aspects of the cycle and cycling.

Newspapers and Magazines

Apart from Club magazines the following are on sale
through newsagents:
Cycling (Weekly) ⎫
Cyclist (Monthly) ⎭ both IPC
Cycling World (Monthly) Stone Publications
Bicycle Times (Monthly) Kelthorn Ltd
Bicycle Magazine (Monthly) Bicycle Magazine

Films

Social secretaries of cycling clubs may find the following useful (videos are available in some cases):
1. *The Stars and the Water Carriers* 1973 Tour of
   Italy with Eddy Merckx (90min. colour)
2. *The Impossible Hour* Ole Ritter's attempt on the
   hour record, Mexico City, 1975 (49min.)
3. *Sunday in Hell* 1976 Paris–Roubaix
4. *Tribute to Tommy Simpson*
5. *Spinning Wheels* features Fausto Coppi, the
   1952 World Championships and the British
   cyclists Vic Gibbons and Eileen Sheridan.
6. *Awheel in Britain* Tour of Britain 1953.

For hire charges and full details, contact: Ray Pascoe,
Flat 1, 57 Crystal Palace Road, East Dulwich, London
SE22.

Two films available from the Department of Trans-
port are:
Cycling Routes in Peterborough
Freewheeling
Contact: Dept of Transport, 2 Marsham Street, Lon-
don SW1P 3EB.

The British Cycling Bureau (BCB) have made a
film on all aspects of cycling (22 min.). Contact: BCB,

Starley House, Eaton Road, Coventry, Warwickshire.

531 The Winner is available on free loan from: Publicity Officer, TI Reynolds Ltd, PO Box 232, Hay Hall, Redfern Road, Birmingham B11 2BG ☎ 021-706 3333. It features top racing at amateur and professional level in 1979.

Cycling: Still the Greatest This film portrays road and track racing of the 1976 Canadian Olympics, and the 1978 Commonwealth Games (27 min.). Contact: National Film Board of Canada, 1 Grosvenor Square, London W1X 0AB.

The Youth Hostels Association (qv) have some general hostelling films which include cycling.

See also: RoSPA

(i) *'Betcher'* – Cycling competition between rival groups.

(ii) *'Wheels of Chance'* – Encourages entry to the Cycling Proficiency Scheme; features Jackie Stewart.

A film for children on a similar theme is: *'Ready for the Road'*, available from the Government Central Film Library.

12

VETERAN CYCLES

Few old machines attract as much attention on the road as early bicycles. And particularly when the riders are wearing period dress.

Most bicycle books of a general nature introduce the subject with a chapter on the history of cycling and include drawings or photographs of early machines, thus giving the reader an excellent first look at veteran cycles.

The enthusiast may develop his interest via two other sources: veteran cycle clubs and museums. There are a number of vigorous Veteran Cycle Clubs and these are listed below (see also the National Association of Veteran Cycle Clubs (NAVCC) and its associated clubs, Chapter 1):

Belton Museum Veteran Cycle Club (see Museums, below)

Benson Veteran Cycle Club C. N. Passey, 61 The Bungalow, Brook Street, Benson, Oxfordshire

Boston Veteran Cycle Club P. Bates, 15 Roseberry Avenue, Boston, Lincolnshire

Bygone Bykes, Yorkshire J. W. Auty, 85 Priory Road, Featherstone, Pontefract, Yorkshire

Desford Lane Pedallers VCC Desford Lane, Leicester

Long Sutton & District VCC P. Shirtcliffe, Hill-crest, Crowhall, Denver, Downham Market, Norfolk

Peterborough Vintage CC Miss Young, 48 Newark Avenue, Peterborough

Roadfarers Veteran CC A. C. Mundy, 22 High
Street, Laister, Peterborough
Southern Veteran CC Mrs A. Green, The Gate-
house, Duns Tew, Oxfordshire

Museums

In addition to machines owned by private enthusiasts,
there are many museums which have one or more
veteran bicycles on display. The most important of
these are:
Beaulieu National Motor Museum This museum
has nine machines which serve as an introduction to
the motorcycle gallery. They span the few years 1867–
1885 and include a Michaux boneshaker and several
ordinaries.
Palace House, Beaulieu, Hampshire ☎ 0590 612345.
Belfast Transport Museum, Witham Street, New-
townards Road, Belfast, Northern Ireland ☎ 0232
51519.
Belton National Cycle Museum This museum looks
set to be the finest collection in Britain, acquiring the
GPO collection, Lord Montagu's collection, the Nash
collection and most of the Science Museum's
machines. A 'living' museum it involves the Belton
House Veteran Cycle Club who ride many of its wide
range of bicycles in the superb park and surrounding
rural area.
Curator: Ray Fixter, Belton House, Grantham, Lin-
colnshire NG32 2LW ☎ 0476 66116.
Birmingham Museum of Science and Industry,
Newhall Street, Birmingham 3 ☎ 021 2361022.
Cheddar Cheddar Motor & Transport Museum,
Cliffe Street, Cheddar, Somerset ☎ 0934 742446.
Coventry Museum of British Road Transport This

Museum has nearly 200 cycles, some dating as far back as 1820.

Cook Street, Coventry, Warwickshire ☎ 0203 25555.

Glasgow   Museum of Transport, 25 Albert Drive, Glasgow G41 ☎ 041 4238000.

Harlow   Just off the A414 road between Bishop's Stortford and Epping, this museum, started by an enthusiast, includes Velocipedes from 1860 and a wooden ordinary of 1869; also a collection of accessories, for example oil and acetylene lamps.

Curator: John Collins, Mark Hall Cycle Museum, Muskham Road, Harlow, Essex ☎ 0279 39680.

Leicester   Leicestershire Museum of Technology, Abbey Pumping Station, Corporation Street, Leicester ☎ 0533 61330.

London   Science Museum, Exhibition Road, South Kensington, London SW7 5DD ☎ 01-589 6371.

Old Warden   The Shuttleworth Collection, Old Warden Aerodrome, Old Warden, Bedfordshire ☎ 076 727288.

Snowshill   Snowshill Manor, Broadway, Worcestershire.

Wrexham   Superb display of vintage cycles in the stables of a National Trust property, 1½ miles south of Wrexham on the A483.

Erddig Hall, Wrexham, Clwyd, Wales ☎ 0978 55314.

INDEX